Web's pulse  *proximity, a increasingly Kendall was woman.*

Last night, as he'd gone over contingency plans, he hadn't anticipated this kind of reaction. But then, he hadn't considered he'd have to hold her this closely, or that the top of her head seemed made to fit under his chin.

Or that her skin would be so soft.

Or that her conversation would be so impertinent, intriguing and intelligent.

Web's friends would have found his situation comical. He didn't, though.

Nor did he think it ironic that the first woman he'd been attracted to in a long time believed he might kill her.

Available in September 2005
from Silhouette Intrigue

Hijacked
Honeymoon

SUSAN KEARNEY

SILHOUETTE®
INTRIGUE™

First published in Great Britain 2005
Silhouette Books, Eton House, 18-24 Paradise Road,
Richmond, Surrey TW9 1SR

© Susan Hope Kearney 2004

ISBN 0 373 22808 2

46-0905

Printed and bound in Spain
by Litografia Rosés S.A., Barcelona

SUSAN KEARNEY

used to set herself on fire four times a day; now she does something really hot—she writes romantic suspense. While she no longer performs her signature fire dive (she's taken up figure skating), she never runs out of ideas for characters and plots. A business graduate from the University of Michigan, Susan is working on her next novel and writes full-time. She resides in a small town outside Tampa, Florida, with her husband and children, and a spoiled Boston terrier.

Visit her at www.SusanKearney.com.

RELAYED MESSAGE:

The SHEY GROUP is a private paramilitary organisation headed by Logan Kincaid. These operatives take on high-risk, high-stakes missions in accord with US government policy. All members are former CIA, FBI or military operatives with top-level security clearances and specialised skills. Members maintain close ties to the underground intelligence network and conduct high-level, behind-the-scenes operations for the government as well as private clients and corporations.

The US government will disavow any connection to SHEY GROUP operations. Employ at your own risk.

CAST OF CHARACTERS

Web Garfield—Ex-CIA agent and mission specialist, Web has been assigned by the Shey Group's legendary founder, Logan Kincaid, to kidnap and protect Kendall Davis—even if that means preventing her from attending her own wedding.

Kendall Davis—Kidnapped from her wedding by a stranger, Kendall is unsure whether she can trust the devastatingly handsome Web Garfield, who claims she's in danger. Suddenly her life is not what it seems, as secrets from her past catch up with her.

Christopher Davis—The genius father Kendall has never met. However, the brilliant scientist has unwittingly placed his daughter in jeopardy.

Beth Patterson—A television newscaster and Kendall's best friend, Beth stirs up a hornet's nest of publicity when her friend goes missing.

Nate Ryson—Ex-Special Forces, Nate holds a longtime grudge against Web. But is he also working against his country?

Franklin Whitelaw—An FBI agent and Kendall's fiancé, Franklin is frantic to find his hijacked bride. But is his concern genuine, or does he have a duplicitous motive?

Chapter One

The mission sucked.

Usually Logan Kincaid, the Shey Group's boss, had merely to name an objective and the team clamored for mission assignments. Not this time. No one had volunteered. So a computer program had spit out Web Garfield's number, and he'd drawn the short straw.

As an ex-CIA agent and hand-to-hand martial arts specialist, Web was prepared emotionally, mentally and physically to take on dangerous missions. He didn't mind risking his life. He didn't mind breaking the law. He didn't mind working in Alabama. But targeting a woman didn't sit right with him—especially a bride on her wedding day.

Taking his gaze off the Gulf of Mexico coastline, Web scowled at Donovan, then ignored the smirk on the other man's face. Although the pilot hadn't taunted him outright, Web didn't have to hear him say the words to know what the other man was thinking. The mission sucked. But after abducting the bride, the pilot could go home to his very pregnant wife, while Web had to baby-sit his abductee—

not exactly a manly challenge. Web barely refrained from gnashing his teeth.

However, Web's self-disgust wouldn't prevent him from completing his mission or from doing it to the best of his ability. Since the boss didn't take on a mission without checking the particulars, and Web's trust in Kincaid was absolute, Web accepted that Kincaid believed the job was necessary, vital and for the common good.

Still, although success might be critical to the future of the United States economy, Web didn't merely dislike his orders, he detested them. Preying on an innocent woman wasn't his thing. He liked his women soft, cuddly and willing, and he always treated the other sex with respect—or he had…until now.

With a sigh of frustration, Web resigned himself to carrying out his objective and moving on. Speaking through a headset, Web Garfield didn't have to raise his voice for the chopper pilot to hear him over the beat of the rotors, the roar of the engine or the whistle of the wind. "What's our ETA?"

"Five minutes." Jack Donovan didn't bother to check his watch. Not only was he the Shey Group's best pilot, the man had a clock inside his head that always ticked on schedule. "Relax. I'll drop you in on time."

The aircraft's engine purred like a well-fed cat, but between the updraft from the cool water of the Gulf of Mexico and the August storm front approaching, air pockets made the chopper pitch, sway and dip. Donovan rode his seat with the ease of a jockey on a galloping racehorse. Jack might have been the best damn pilot in the entire air force, but to him a smooth flight and landing meant that no one died.

Resigned, Web slouched in his seat and swallowed hard. He wasn't uncomfortable in the air, but he preferred to keep his feet on terra firma, where a man relied on his brain and muscles—not a tin can wrapped around a motor to keep him alive.

Automatically, Web gave Donovan a hard time, but his heart wasn't in it. "Yeah, well I'd like to set down with my lunch still *inside* my stomach."

"Hey, don't blame me for a little air turbulence." Donovan checked his instruments. "We don't have time to fly around the storm." Web couldn't help noting the glee in Donovan's voice. The man was born to fly. The storm was simply a challenge he enjoyed as much as Web did a good karate match in the *dojo* or a demanding mission.

Web shrugged the tension out of his shoulders and peered through the windshield into the storm. Waiting, the time before the action was always the hard part, the time where doubts crept in and could bite a man if he wasn't careful. Once they landed, he'd click into fighting mode and the mental preparation would kick in. He'd no longer question the mission, but simply focus on getting the job done in the minimum amount of time with the least hassle.

Lightning flashed, zigzagging in a spectacular display of nature's fury. Dark clouds closed down on the earth like a hulking army, and the slashing rain lowered visibility to less than five feet. As the lightning bolts electrified the air around them, beside Web, Donovan didn't flinch and relied on his instruments. Web remained as stoic and tried not to think about his target as a woman—impossible, of course.

She would be furious, no doubt. What woman wouldn't be angry, scared and upset over being abducted by strangers less than an hour before her *I do*s? What woman would believe a stranger was kidnapping her to protect her? Web expected a flood of tears, heart-wrenching sobs, begging. And he damned the program that had spit out his name. However, the thought of refusing hadn't crossed his mind but for a second. It wasn't simply that the Shey Group paid him so well, or that Web had more respect for Logan Kincaid than almost anyone else he knew. Men like Web didn't complain when they drew point. They didn't complain when the risk of success approached absolute zero. The Shey Group didn't complain period. Complaining was for wimps.

To avoid eyewitnesses, the timing with the local law enforcement—who had no idea why the Shey Group had requested the interstate be shut down for ten minutes—had to go off like clockwork. Not an easy feat, considering the mission had been planned only last night. A temporary roadblock would isolate the bride's limousine. Kincaid had expertly inserted one of the Shey Group into the limo as a replacement driver, so the extraction could take place without witnesses.

The target would be alone. Vulnerable. Scared.

If Web had been in charge of planning, he would have knocked on her door, made an explanation and asked her to cooperate, but Kincaid said they simply couldn't take the risk that she wouldn't be alone or that she might refuse to help them. After all, her loyalty would belong to the man she was about to marry. The man waiting at the altar for his bride—

a bride whom Web had to ensure wouldn't show for her nuptials.

About to spoil what she likely expected to be the happiest day of her life, Web cracked his knuckles, glaring as wind knocked the aircraft into a sideways slide. Landing would be like threading a needle while riding a bucking bronco, yet he had confidence in Donovan. Last year the man had successfully landed in the middle of a blizzard in the Rockies. If anyone could get them in and out fast, he could. Web had no doubts about his partner's skill or his own to do what must be done. But he didn't have to like it.

"Locked on target." Donovan pointed to the sleek white limousine, already pulled onto the highway's shoulder, right next to a large patch of grass. "Perfect. No phone wires. No trees. No eyewitnesses."

Just one helluva storm. Web kept the thought to himself. Right about now, the driver would be pretending to call for a tow truck and assuring the lovely bride that despite the engine trouble, she'd still make it to her wedding on time.

She wouldn't, of course. Web's job was to make sure she wouldn't.

Before Jack set down, Web had unfastened his seat belt, removed the headset and opened his door. He jumped out, letting his knees absorb the shock of the landing, then sprinted straight for the limousine.

The downpour drenched him within two footsteps. The soggy turf sucked at his boots. But a little rain and mud wouldn't slow Web's determined strides.

He reached the limo's door, and the woman inside

peered through the rain at him. A vision in white, her green eyes narrowed in suspicion, her perfectly made-up face contrasted with white skin pale from shock as she stared at him in confusion.

She must have seen something on Web's face that she didn't like. Slamming her palm down on the lock in one decisive move, she shouted to the driver. Thunder boomed and reverberated, and Web couldn't hear her words, but when from up front the driver unlocked the doors, her slicing look of anger and hurt and bewilderment stabbed him.

Yet his finer feelings didn't stop him from yanking open the door. He steeled himself for her tears. When a shoe slammed into his face, the spiky hee coming close to poking out his eye but sliding past his temple instead, and leaving a painful, bloody furrow, her bold attitude took him by surprise. Ignoring his injury, leaning inside, he grabbed for her waist and barely dropped his chin in time to avoid a well-placed kick to his throat.

"Lady, I don't want to hurt you."

As if she hadn't heard him, she scratched and swore words no Southern belle should know, never mind utter, and scooted backward, her legs kicking, her dress riding up to reveal toned calves and trim ankles. He grabbed a handful of white satin and hauled her toward the open door. Needing to grab her, not the damn dress, he felt past the voluminous material, and his hand grazed a slender hip before she squirmed out of reach.

"My fiancé works for the FBI," she yelled at him. "And if you know what's good for you—" finally, his fingers grasped her tiny waist and he hauled her out of the car into the fierce rain ''—you'll let me go.''

She whacked him across the nose with her purse, followed up with a fist to his ear. ''Bastard. Get your hands off me.''

Web didn't release her but swore under his breath. ''Lady, I don't want to hit you, but if you don't stop fighting, you'll give me no choice.''

She didn't waste her breath screaming. Redoubling her efforts, she paid no attention to his plea to be reasonable or to the rain soaking her and causing her makeup to run until her eyes resembled a raccoon's. Even if she cooperated, which didn't seem likely, no way could she walk across the muddy ground in those spiky shoes. Already the rain weighed down her dress, hampering her movements, but that didn't prevent her from twisting and snarling like a wild cat.

Despite his threat otherwise, unwilling to deck her and mar her delicate skin or worse risk breaking her jaw, Web picked her up, tossed her over his shoulder. He ran through the rain back to the chopper, ignoring her fists pounding his back, her knees kicking his ribs, but very aware of his hand on her pleasantly curved bottom.

Web climbed into the chopper, holding the wet and squirming woman. ''Go, Jack.''

''We're out of here.''

''Stop,'' she shouted over the roar of the engine. ''I'll give you money.''

The time for explanation had arrived. Web let her slide down his chest, keeping her too close to wind up for a punch or a kick, trying and failing not to notice her sexy curves. "Kendall, we're not interested in money."

HE KNOWS MY NAME.

Before Kendall Davis had a second to analyze the ramifications of that statement, the helicopter lifted into the air. However, the man who'd manhandled her had finally released her and the door was still open.

Kendall didn't hesitate, she lunged toward the opening, preferring to suffer a five- to ten-foot drop than whatever these two guys had in mind for her. What she'd do after she hit the ground she had no idea. The limo driver must have been in on... whatever the hell was going on.

She'd figure that out later. First, she had to flee. And if that meant plunging out of the helicopter, she'd find a way to roll after she hit the ground.

"No, you don't." From behind, a muscular arm wrapped around her throat and dragged her back against a powerful chest.

She yelped in frustration as the wet and heavy dress hindered her movements. When he didn't cut off her flow of air, she stomped on his foot, but her heel missed and her high arch of her shoe did little damage. Kendall slammed her head back, trying to break his nose, but her head only reached his chest and that thick arm of his tightened under her chin, pinning her head back, arching her spine.

She jammed an elbow into his gut, hoping he'd collapse with an oof of air. But her leverage was at a bad angle and her elbow struck muscle so solid and dense he might as well have been wearing armor. So much for her limited self-defense moves.

Obviously, she should have taken a class instead of ordering a tape. But just because she couldn't match the man physically didn't mean she was out of options. Kendall's life had rarely been easy and giving up wasn't part of her vocabulary, although she was stymied at the moment.

"Stop fighting me," he ordered, his tone businesslike, and if she hadn't known better, sounding almost sympathetic, even if he had shouted to be heard over the wind and engines. With his free hand he pulled the door shut and twisted a lock, but a glance out the windshield revealed that another try would be suicidal. They must have been fifty feet off the ground and climbing.

Where were they going?

He straightened without releasing her. With her head tilted back, she had a view of his corded neck, mountained shoulders and stubborn jaw. He snagged a headset from the wall and jammed it over her ears, did the same for himself, all without releasing his hold.

His voice came through the headset, brisk yet gentle. "If I let go, will you promise—"

She tugged at the arm across her throat. "I'm not promising you a thing."

His arm didn't budge. "I'm not here to hurt you—"

"You already have." She pried his pinky loose, attempted to bend it back. "You ruined my dress, my hair, my makeup and now I'm late for my wedding. You damn well better have a good reason for…" She stopped trying to bend his pinky, which was stronger than her entire hand. Fighting had been instinctive when she'd been unable to flee in the limo that she now suspected hadn't overheated as the driver had claimed. Her brain hadn't really kicked in until now. But nothing had made sense since her driver had pulled over along the deserted highway. Women disappeared from parking lots. Or from bars. They didn't get kidnapped by helicopter.

This wasn't some abduction by a psycho, but an organized operation conducted by three men. The driver, her captor and the pilot. And a helicopter was expensive. Kendall didn't rate this kind of attention. She wasn't that special.

Tipping up her eyes, she tried to watch her captor. "Did Franklin Whitelaw send you?"

As she thought of her fiancé waiting alone at the altar and having to excuse her unexplainable absence to their guests, her fury rose. Yet perhaps these men worked for the FBI. That would explain the chopper, the limo, the lack of traffic on the road that had let them abduct her without witnesses. But it didn't explain his hold on her neck or his manhandling her.

Finally the man released her. "It's because of Franklin that we're here."

"You're FBI?" She turned around to face him, taking in the wary eyes, the big hands ready to grab her again if she made one wrong move.

He shook his head, calling attention to a wound at his temple that was bleeding profusely, mixing with the rain and painting one side of his face red. She didn't feel the least bit sorry for the damage she'd caused—she actually wished she could have done enough to stop them from abducting her. But now that she had a better look at him, she realized she hadn't stood a chance. At six feet tall, the man had the musculature of a professional wrestler. Big arms, big legs, big hands, big everything.

Wearing dark jeans and a dark shirt, he could have stepped out of the pages of *People* magazine's issue depicting the top fifty sexiest men. He had a bold jaw, wide-set eyes and commanding cheekbones. And a don't-toy-with-me expression.

She didn't understand why they'd gone to all the trouble to take her. She was a nobody, a temp, working odd jobs to make ends meet as she put herself through community college. However, Franklin was an FBI agent, in accounting, he'd told her. Since his excuses about why he often disappeared for days didn't always add up, she'd suspected her fiancé worked undercover and had been unable to tell her more about his real assignments. But she'd never questioned him too closely, knowing that after 9/11 the government had stepped up security throughout the country.

"Is Franklin all right?"

The man reached into his pocket, pulled out a bandanna and secured it over the wound as casually as Franklin knotted his tie. "Well, I'd imagine he's a little perturbed that his bride didn't show up, embarrassed at having to explain your absenteeism and miffed that he hasn't a clue what happened to you, but otherwise, he's fine." The man who had legs as thick as tree trunks and arms to match looked at her with quiet gray eyes. "I'm Web Garfield. The pilot is Jack Donovan."

Why would he tell her his name? If she got free she could go straight to the authorities. Did he intend to kill her? Was that why he didn't care if she knew who they were? But she sensed if he'd wanted to kill her she'd already be dead.

Had these men kidnapped her to get to Franklin? If so, they'd planned with care. With no bride's room at the old church, she'd donned her wedding dress at home. Normally her maid of honor, Beth Patterson, would have ridden with her. But one of Beth's hobbies was flower arranging and she had agreed to set up the flowers at the church. These men had probably picked the only moment all day that Kendall wouldn't be with someone else. That kind of planning took brains and skill to carry off—which brought her right back to the idea that these men needed her to get to her fiancé.

Were they going to ask Franklin to give up some vital information in exchange for her? Shoving her wet hair from her eyes, she glanced from Web to the pilot, reminding herself that terrorists came in all shapes and sizes—because these two were a pair of the best-looking men she'd seen in a long time. Especially Web, the dark-eyed Conan-the-Barbarian type with the gentle voice, who had gone out of his way not to hurt her, despite her struggles.

"What do you want with me? Where are we going?"

"The explanations will have to wait," the pilot, Jack, interrupted, his tone firm. "Get her in a seat and both of you strap in."

"Problem?" Web asked, shoving her firmly but gently into a seat and fastening the belt across her lap, his hands smooth and efficient despite their huge size.

She didn't fight him. What was the point? She'd

lost her chance to flee out the door until they landed again.

"We're going down."

The pilot didn't sound particularly perturbed, but she got the impression from his tone that they weren't making a scheduled landing.

"What do you mean, we're going down?" she asked, fear pumping adrenaline into her veins. But there was no one to fight. No place to run.

"Don't worry. Jack's good." If Web's words were meant to reassure her, they had the opposite effect. His tone was tight as he slid into the seat next to her and behind the pilot. "What's wrong?" she asked, but then the motors cut out, making the answer to her question all too obvious.

As the pilot calmly flipped a few buttons, pumped the pedals with his feet and adjusted the stick control with his right hand, her heart hammered her ribs and her pulse thudded. When they didn't immediately plunge to the earth, she prayed for the pilot to restart the engines.

He didn't. Or couldn't. But unlike a jet plane that lost momentum and dived into the earth, the chopper fell in fits and starts. The overhead blades still turned, keeping them from a completely out-of-control crash.

Perhaps this might be her chance to escape. If the chopper went down…she needed to get out, run. But she had no idea where they were. She saw no lights below. It looked as if the storm had swallowed up all signs of civilization.

They swooped, spinning at crazy angles, the storm buffeting the craft, the rain slicing against the windshield. All thoughts of escape fled. While the pilot worked his controls, her mind flashed over the reality that surviving the upcoming crash seemed impossible. Not with the tall trees below. Not with the chopper plunging first to one side then somersaulting to the other until she lost track of up and down and her gut felt like she was on a roller coaster that had jumped its tracks.

"I'm autorotating down."

"Jack?" Web's voice was smooth, as if absolutely nothing were wrong.

"Yeah?" Jack worked the controls, seemingly having no trouble talking and handling the emergency. "Got your seat backs and tray tables in their upright positions?"

"Cute."

The craft swooped, rolled.

"Oh, God." Kendall clutched the arms of her seat.

She didn't want to die. She wasn't afraid of death, not after nursing her mother through the cancer that had taken her last year. For her mother, death had been a blessing after so much suffering and pain. She'd been ready to go—but Kendall wasn't. There were too many things she wanted to do.

She wanted to marry Franklin and finish college. She wanted to buy that sweet little house in the mountains. She wanted time to do more than struggle through life. Ever since her father had abandoned her mother when Kendall was a baby, first her mother, then Kendall had fought to make ends meet. Her mother had worked in a hair salon during the day, bagged groceries at night and cleaned houses on the weekends. Kendall had baby-sat and worked temp jobs all through high school and had earned a college scholarship to Alabama. But then her mom had gotten sick and Kendall returned home to take care of the woman who'd devoted her life to her only daughter. Kendall had promised her mother that she would finish her interrupted education and Franklin had agreed, which was one of the reasons she'd said yes to his sudden proposal. Kendall longed for some stability in her life. She longed for family. She wanted to live.

Beside her, Web reached out, took her hand, held on tight and joked with the pilot. "Kincaid isn't going to be happy if you ditch another chopper."

Gallows humor. Who were these guys? Who was Kincaid?

"Hey, it wasn't my fault the chopper in Tampa had a bomb on it."

A bomb?

"Is it true, Kincaid can't get insurance on you?"

"Naw. I'm expensive as hell, but that's because I'm damn good."

Kendall would have rolled her eyes upward at the macho BS, if she'd known which direction up was. "If you're so damn good, you'd better get us down in one piece."

"Yes, ma'am. If I don't, my wife Piper will not be…" Something in the cockpit sizzled, smoked. Jack flipped switches, and several of his instruments that had been lit turned dark. "Sorry about that, folks."

"What happened?" Web asked, still holding her hand.

Despite the fact that the man had kidnapped her, she couldn't seem to snatch her hand back. Not with the storm thundering around them, the rain slashing and the craft pitching like a cork in a shark-infested sea.

"You don't want to know." Jack started to whistle.

Outside, lightning flashed, and she saw treetops through the windshield, but no clear patches. No place safe to set down. That was assuming the pilot could still steer, something she doubted as she coughed on the smoke.

"Brace for impact," Jack instructed.

Beside her, Web pushed her head down, then grabbed her hand again. "We'll be fine. Jack was born under a lucky star or his wife would never have married him."

"How comforting." Kendall beat down her fear, wishing she had something to do, something to keep her mind occupied. With her head down, she caught sight of the watch on her wrist. Five o'clock. She was supposed to be marrying Franklin, saying her vows in a church filled with neighbors and friends—not crashing in a helicopter with two men who'd swooped out of the sky and abducted her.

Kendall didn't even have nightmares this bad.

She wanted to scream, but her throat was too tight with fear. During her mother's illness, she kept her hands busy cooking and sewing and doing collages to push back the tight ache in her chest from constant grief. She'd read so many books, many of them aloud so her mother could enjoy them, too. Waiting for the impact would have been easier if she'd had something to occupy her mind other than thoughts of disaster. If she had to die, she prayed it would be quick, painless.

Jack chuckled. "Landing site to the right."

Web squeezed her hand. "Hang on."

These guys had to be either the bravest men she knew—or crazy. Kendall caught sight of trees. Branches at odd angles.

In moments they would be down. Or dead.

Chapter Two

Web told himself he held Kendall's hand to prevent her from trying to flee after they landed. But he knew better. Beside the guilt that stabbed him for interrupting her wedding and then placing her into a mechanically unsound aircraft, he liked holding her hand, needed that human touch from her as much as he sensed she needed it from him.

If they were about to die, rather than clinging to cold metal, he'd rather go with her warm flesh in his. To say that Kendall had shocked him would have been an understatement. He hadn't expected her to fight bravely, or to stop when she obviously couldn't escape after the chopper had reached a high altitude. Most women in Kendall's situation would have been screaming or crying as the chopper plummeted, but she'd remained silent, containing her fear to allow Jack to concentrate on flying.

For someone totally out of her element, she was acting like a pro—with courage and smarts that he admired. And that made him feel even worse for spoiling her wedding day. For some reason he'd expected a Southern bimbo to be marrying Franklin—

not a smart, brave woman. Web hoped his actions weren't about to get her killed.

In theory, Jack should have no trouble landing without the engine. However, that theory didn't take into account the storm, the lack of a level landing site or that the chopper had likely been sabotaged. Kincaid paid whatever it took for top-notch mechanics and the latest equipment. And Jack had meticulously gone over the craft before they'd taken off. Although mechanical failure was possible, Web's gut told him that someone dangerous had caught up with them.

Despite their efforts, had Franklin gotten wind of the operation through his extensive network of contacts in the FBI? Had he sent someone to sabotage the aircraft in an attempt to cover his tracks and continue his traitorous scheme? Could he have planned for the chopper to go down *before* Web had kidnapped his bride but had miscalculated so the engines had failed later than expected? There were too many unknowns, and Web wished they could break radio silence. But Kincaid had warned them that with Franklin's FBI contacts, they had to fly under the radar to avoid detection and to stay off the radio and cell phones.

And now they were rocking, bumping, grinding. With the way they pitched through the gusting wind, it would be a miracle if Jack got them down. But Web had flown with Jack before and he had seen him perform the impossible. The pilot had a sixth sense, a seat-of-his-pants altimeter inside him. Somehow, Jack could feel the land coming up to meet them, a sense that made the burned-out instruments on the control panel unnecessary.

The chopper slammed forward, then back. With his head down, his feet braced, Web's shoulder smacked into the wall. His seat's frame yanked out of the floor with a screech of stressed metal and he skidded into Kendall's seat. But he figured they were down and released the air he'd been holding in his lungs. Then they dropped again.

"Hold on," Jack ordered.

"Like I'm going to let go," Web muttered.

The last ten feet seemed to go by in slow motion. Web's stomach surged into his throat. Although knowing his muscles would be no match for the velocity and mass of steel dive-bombing the earth with incalculable forces, he clamped one hand onto the seat in front of him.

The landing came as a shock. After the bone-snapping bouncing and jarring of the aircraft, Jack set them down on the landing struts with barely a tap.

"Nice job," he complimented the pilot, then turned to Kendall. "You okay?"

"Just peachy," she muttered sarcastically, her face pale, her hands shaking.

"We've got a fuel leak that's trouble." Jack flipped switches and his tone deepened with urgency. "Get out. Now."

As if his warning needed emphasizing, Jack kicked out the windshield. The Plexiglas popped with a noisy release of suction. Wind and rain and the reek of burning fuel roared into the chopper. Jack scrambled out the front, disappearing into the weather.

Web unlocked his seat belt, opened the rear door

and turned to help Kendall. Right behind him, she didn't require his help.

Web leaped to the ground. Rain slashed him, and he prayed the storm would put out the fire from the explosion he sensed was coming. He'd hate to survive a chopper crash only to burn in a forest fire.

One emergency at a time.

Kendall landed right next to him but, unbalanced, she almost fell. Grabbing her hand, he tugged her away from the chopper. "Run."

She swore at her shoes, reminding him of those impractical spiked heels. Walking in them on pavement would have been difficult. In the rain, in a forest, running was practically impossible. And to add to her difficulties, her bridal gown was wet, heavy.

She bent to take off the shoes.

"No time." Web swept her into his arms. And ran like hell.

This time she didn't fight him. She wrapped her arms around his neck, buried her head against his chest and clung tightly. He should have smelled her scent, but instead, the odor of fuel and smoke urged his feet faster.

"Over here." From behind a downed tree, Jack waved him closer.

They'd almost reached Jack, who'd dashed out from behind cover to help him, when the chopper exploded. Caught in the concussing blast, the three of them tumbled, Jack and Web automatically rolling for cover, tugging Kendall with them. Both men covered her with their bodies as metal, flames and fuel burst from the aircraft.

"I can't breathe." Kendall squirmed beneath him. Web lifted most of his weight from her. Jack rolled away, leaving him to deal with her. Her white gown was now not only wet but filthy, as dirt, leaves and debris clung to the wet material. But the steady downpour of rain had already wiped most of the makeup from her face, leaving her looking younger and appearing more vulnerable with her blond hair slicked to her head.

With the immediate danger over, Web released her. "Sorry. You okay, ma'am?"

"Yeah."

All three of them climbed to their feet and stared at the burning chopper. Web glanced at Jack. "Time for Plan B."

"Plan B?" Kendall asked. "What exactly was Plan A?"

Web frowned, much more on his mind than answering her question. With flames shooting up from the downed aircraft, every satellite focused on the southern part of the U.S. would pick up the heat and their trail. Traveling with Kendall would be slow—even if she cooperated—and that was far from a given. So he stalled, thinking, planning, only willing to say so much. "Kincaid's not going to be happy about the chopper."

Jack shoved hair off his forehead. "I'm not worried about Kincaid. I promised Piper I'd be home today."

"Then get going. I'll take care of Kendall."

At his words, Kendall backed away, mumbling something about taking care of herself. Web didn't try to stop her. She wouldn't get far in those shoes and heavy dress. Besides, he wanted to say a few words to Jack without her overhearing.

"You sure?" Jack asked.

"Go. Your wife needs you."

The two men shook hands.

"Okay," Jack agreed, then turned up his collar against the rain. Per standard operating procedure, he didn't ask which direction Web planned to go. In case Jack was questioned, he wouldn't be able to give away Web's location. On the other hand, he also wouldn't be able to tell Kincaid where Web was. But that was fine. Kincaid gave his men room to operate and right now, Web intended to take advantage of that modus operandi.

"Jack, when's the baby due?" Web asked.

Jack grinned. "Babies don't come according to a reliable ETA. Why?"

"You have time to lay a false trail to the south and buy us some time?"

"No problem."

No problem for him, maybe. Web still had to talk to Kendall, who was fleeing through the woods. She'd chosen to go north. He supposed that direction was as good as any.

KENDALL CONCENTRATED on putting as much distance between herself and her kidnappers as possible. She didn't understand why they had let her go, but prayed that the downed chopper had caused them to give up their initial plans for her. Perhaps they were set on fleeing before the authorities arrived to check out the chopper crash—that was assuming anyone knew the aircraft had gone down. Between the storm and the isolated area, she couldn't count on any witnesses. As usual, she'd have to rely on herself.

Kendall considered losing the gown, but the prospect of running through the woods in her underwear, her tender flesh exposed to mosquitoes and who knew what kind of bugs was even less appealing than hauling the oversize skirt over muddy ground. However, she did stop to remove her slip and crinoline, tossing the useless clothing aside. Unfortunately, the action didn't lighten her load too much. The mud at her hemline added to the weight of the soggy dress, but she kept trudging, then had to stop again when her heel caught in a hole and she tripped.

She removed her white satin shoes in the hope of altering them. Using all her strength she attempted to break off the heel like she'd seen in the movie *Romancing the Stone*. But either her shoes were made better than the ones in the movie, or she lacked the necessary force. Going barefoot wasn't a good option. Not in the mud where she couldn't see exactly where her feet were going. She'd lived in Alabama long enough to know that a downpour such as this brought out the snakes from their normal hiding places.

If she wasn't careful, she could walk right into a swamp. Although she'd traveled at no more than a fast walk, her heart sped as if she'd completed a sprint. She was lost in a forest of oak and hickory, with a possible killer on her trail, wearing the most ridiculous clothing.

Think positive.

She wasn't dead. Not even hurt. And she'd escaped from her captors. All she had to do was find a road, a cabin, a hunter and she could be back in civilization within the hour. Wishing she'd paid more attention to their location while she'd still been in the air, she put the heels back on and tried to decide which direction to go.

As she glanced left, right and back over her shoulder, she couldn't miss Web's massive silhouette outlined against the dying flames of the chopper. Damn. She should have known a man like him wouldn't give up on the mission after a setback. Jack was nowhere to be seen, and she didn't know if having only Web to contend with made her feel better or worse.

There was no point in trying to outrun him, so she turned and faced him. Hoping he hadn't decided to kill her off, she stooped and picked up a good-size branch and held it at her side. No way could she win a physical fight with this man, but that didn't mean she'd cave.

"How far can you walk in those shoes?" Web asked, his voice gentle.

She didn't allow the kindness in his tone to dull her vigilance. Alone in the woods, she could shout and no one would hear her. This man could do whatever he wanted to her, so no sympathetic tone would alleviate her distress.

If he intended to head farther from the crash site to kill her and hide her body, she didn't intend to help him. Unsure of his reason for asking the question, she hesitated, then answered vaguely. "Between my heels and this dress, I don't know how far I can go."

"Let me see the shoes." He held out his hand.

"Why?"

"Because I saw you attempting to break off the heels. You didn't have the proper equipment to do the job. I do."

She frowned at him, unsure what he meant, but some of her fear lessened. "What equipment?"

"Look, we haven't had time to talk, but I won't harm you. Will you freak if I use my pocketknife to cut off the heel of your shoes?"

He didn't reach for her. Or his knife. He stood still, giving her time to think. And she realized if he had just pulled out the knife, she *would* have freaked. But now that he'd given her time to understand his intentions, she realized that if he wanted to kill her, he could do so as easily with his bare hands as a knife.

Praying he wasn't some sicko who liked to inflict pain on women before killing them, she kicked off one shoe, then the other. Still gripping the branch, she used her free hand to toss over her shoes.

"Let's see what I can do." He picked up her shoes, then leaned back against a thick oak, as if deliberately trying to appear nonthreatening. Reaching into a pocket, he removed and opened a wicked-looking pocketknife, held up her shoe and sliced the satin across the heel. "I work for a group of ex-military and CIA types hired by the U.S. Government."

"And you specialize in bride abduction?" The words popped out before she'd thought better. Whenever she was scared, and she was good and frightened, she turned sarcastic, not always the wisest of decisions.

He grinned at her cynical remark. "Actually, extracting you was my first bride hijacking."

He sounded sincere, but the meticulous manner in which he carved her shoe had her convinced of one thing—the man knew how to use a knife. It was almost as if the tool was an extension of his mind. The cuts were sharp, sure, controlled. His hands strong and clever.

If he'd been hired by the government that would explain the use of the helicopter, the military precision of the operation and his disciplined nature. However, she wasn't some Little-Miss-Innocent who'd believe whatever he told her. She tightened her grip on the branch. "You have any proof of what you're telling me?"

"Professionals don't carry ID."

She recalled Franklin's badge. "FBI agents do."

"Not the ones working undercover." With one last deft slice, he flicked off the heel, then examined the bottom, rubbing his thumb over the surface. He must have found a few rough spots because he turned the shoe back over and carved off a few tiny pieces. As if comprehending her reluctance to come closer to him, he tossed her shoe back and began to work on the other. "Here, see if that works better."

She wriggled her foot into her right shoe and tested her balance. "Thanks."

"No problem. You aren't going to like the next part."

"I didn't like the last part, where I missed my wedding, or when the helicopter crashed, either." She sighed. "So why did you abduct me?"

"For your own protection."

"Excuse me?" As far as stories went, his was growing more bizarre by the moment. "I was going to church, to my wedding, where my friends and neighbors intended to share the beginnings of a celebration of my new life as half of a couple. And you want me to believe I needed protection? From whom? My friends and neighbors?''

"This is the part you won't like."

She tried to blow a lock of hair from her eyes in exasperation. But her hair was too wet to budge. So she shoved it aside and ignored the icy trickle down her neck. "Tell me."

"You need protection from the groom."

"Franklin? That's ridiculous. He's an FBI agent." She expected Web to retract his accusation, come up with some other line that might be more believable. He didn't.

"Another government group has had your fiancé under surveillance for quite some time. Apparently, he's a double agent."

"He's an accountant."

"No, he isn't. Franklin lied to you." Web looked up from the shoe and speared her with those level gray eyes. "He's an undercover operative—"

"Working in Alabama? Why?" The whole story sounded ridiculous.

Web held up the second shoe and then sliced a neat cut at the heel joint. "Franklin's plan was to take you out of the country on your honeymoon. I believe you intended to go to Egypt?"

She didn't like how easily Web could make an innocent-sounding honeymoon sound suspicious. "So?"

Web tossed her the other shoe. She moved the stick to her free hand and slipped the shoe on, the motion automatic. Meanwhile, her thoughts raced like a runaway train. Stodgy, dependable Franklin a double agent? She no more believed him capable of that level of deception than she believed Web was telling her everything he knew.

"Franklin wanted to take you out of the country so he and his terrorist buddies could hold you hostage."

"Oh, come on," she protested. Terrorists? Franklin? But *she'd* wanted to go to Niagara Falls for their honeymoon. Franklin had insisted on spending the money for a once-in-a-lifetime vacation. At the time his gesture had seemed romantic, but because Franklin lived frugally and they'd been saving for a down payment on a house, she'd asked him if he'd won the lottery.

As if reading her mind, Web asked, "Whose idea was it to visit Egypt?"

"Maybe Franklin likes adventure. That hardly makes him a double agent. Or in league with terrorists."

"Doesn't an accountant wanting an adventure seem a tad contradictory to you?" Web prodded.

"Perhaps he wanted to make up for his boring work by going somewhere exotic. I thought the idea romantic."

"Did you?"

"Yes. And even if he's what you say—which I don't believe—even if he wanted me to leave the country with him, you haven't explained why." She held up a hand, wondering what Franklin had done and how he'd felt when she hadn't shown up. Had he gotten drunk? Had he cried? Cursed? Was he frantic with worry that something terrible must have happened to her? Even as she and Web spoke, was Franklin using all his influence at the FBI to find her? She simply didn't know. "And don't tell me

I'm not going to like this part. I don't like standing in the rain. I don't like being here with you. And I don't like—''

''What do you know about your father?''

''My father?''

The sudden change in subject threw her off-kilter. She tried not to think about the man who hadn't even stuck around long enough to know if his baby was a boy or a girl. Or how much she'd missed having a dad like the other kids. Or how her mother had never said a bad word against the man who'd left her to raise a baby by herself or allowed Kendall to speak ill of him, either.

From habit she kept the bitterness from her tone. ''My father abandoned my mother when I was an infant.''

She knew next to nothing about the man, except that her mother had claimed he was a brilliant scientist. One who'd preferred his laboratory to his wife or child. Her father's IQ didn't matter one iota to Kendall. Especially since she suspected his emotional intelligence had been no higher than a jackass's. What else could she think? No less than a year after Christopher Davis had married her mother and gotten her pregnant, he'd taken off for parts unknown.

''Could we do two things at once?'' Web asked.

''What?''

''While we have this discussion, with your permission, I'd like to modify your dress.'' At the thought of him becoming her personal tailor, she almost smiled. Then he held up his knife. ''I won't cut you, I promise. But you can't traipse around the woods in that dress. Between the water and the mud, that material must weigh forty pounds.''

As he approached with the knife, she forced her feet to remain still. Although she told herself he wouldn't have bothered to fix her shoes if he now intended to stab her, her heart began to hammer. ''What are you proposing?''

''At least let me slice off the material dragging the ground.''

His words made sense. She kept tripping over the long hemline, but she sensed he wasn't done making suggestions. ''And?''

''If I cut out the excess material in the skirt, I can fashion you some loose slacks.''

''I'll do it myself.'' She held out her hand for the knife.

''I don't think so.''

''Why not?'' She challenged him with her tone.

''If you know how to use the knife, you might attack me. If you don't know what you're doing, you could hurt yourself.''

She raised her eyebrow. ''And you're an expert at altering bridal attire?''

''Oh, I'm good at all kinds of things.''

''Do it, hotshot.'' If he inadvertently helped her to flee by lightening her load, she'd accept. ''And while you're at it, don't forget to tell me what my father has to do with…me.''

Web bent and hacked off the hem of her dress. ''Christopher Davis claims to be inventing an automobile engine that's fueled by hydrogen.''

She so didn't care. ''Isn't that nice.''

''Our government believes his project could lower our country's reliance on imported oil.''

"And?" She had no idea what her father had to do with her and wondered if Web was deliberately stringing her along for some ulterior motive of his own.

"Spread your legs, please."

She closed her eyes, did as he asked and reminded herself that in the deepening darkness, he could see less of her than if she'd worn a swimsuit on a beach. Except they weren't on a beach. The man was kneeling between her legs with a knife mere inches from her flesh, and she shivered.

"Could you drop that branch and hold the material tight? I don't want to risk nicking you."

So he'd noticed her makeshift club. She had to remember that Web was very observant. She supposed in his line of work, whether that was a kidnapper or a mercenary hired by the government, the difference between living and dying might depend on the little details. Dropping the branch, she clenched the material at her thighs and drew it tight.

"What does my father's invention have to do with my own situation?"

Carefully, he inserted the knife point midway between her legs, about eight inches above her knees. With a clean gash downward, he ripped open her dress, cutting out a triangle with the point up and the majority of material removed from the hemline.

"Turn around."

She did as he asked, and he repeated the procedure at the back of the dress. He'd left wide sections to wrap around her legs. In swift, sure movements, he cut holes in her dress along the inside of her legs. Then, using the extra material from the hem, he threaded it through the holes. Considering they were standing in the pouring rain and he was working with drenched material, she was surprised by his success. As promised, she now wore loose pants that weighed a whole lot less than her dress.

"You make a better tailor than a conversationalist."

"Under the circumstances, I'd think you'd understand I was a mite distracted. Just because I'm not going to attack you doesn't mean I don't appreciate the sight of a great pair of legs."

The not-going-to-attack-her comment did little to reassure. The compliment annoyed her and reminded her that Franklin never gave her a compliment like that. For once, she bit down on her temper and steered the subject back where she wanted it to go. "You still haven't explained…"

At the sound of an approaching aircraft, she opened her eyes and looked up. Between the treetops, twin searchlights beamed over the forest. And stopped, centering on a clearing mere yards from where they stood.

Kendall's hopes rose. "We're rescued."

She stepped toward the light, but Web grabbed her shoulder, his fingers tightening, halting her forward momentum. "Don't."

"Someone must have seen us go down." Excited, she tried to twist past him. "That's the Forest Service looking for us."

"Maybe." His grip remained firm, imprisoning her in the shadows.

"See the insignia on the chopper?"

"Maybe the FBI appropriated it. We can't take the risk."

She'd rather depend on the FBI than the stranger

holding her captive in the forest. But her survival instincts kicked in. Since she couldn't argue him out of the notion of remaining hidden, she tried to appear as if she didn't resent his decision.

"Okay," she agreed, hoping her sudden capitulation didn't seem suspicious. Although Web hadn't hurt her, his story made no sense. No way did she believe his wild accusations about Franklin. Yet she also knew that he could easily prevent her from reaching the clearing.

"They will land and advance directly to the burning chopper. When they don't find bodies, they'll call in dogs to track us. The wet ground will work in our favor. Meanwhile, we'll head in the other direction." Web gave her a gentle shove.

"Okay, I'm going." But she walked slowly, picking her moment. And after the chopper landed and cut off the engine, she opened her mouth to scream.

Chapter Three

Web could have angled his mouth over Kendall's to silence her. But however much he might have enjoyed gathering her into his arms and tasting her own brand of Southern sass, he couldn't take advantage of her. She was an innocent target, and he had to keep that first and foremost in mind. So, he gently clamped one hand over her mouth, tugged her against him with the other. With her back pressed to his chest, he didn't have to face the temptation of her smart lips. Or see the accusing anger in her eyes.

She struggled, twisting her full hips against his. She tried to stomp on his foot, kick his shin, ram her elbow into his stomach but he shifted and avoided damage from her attack.

"Stop it," he whispered in her ear. And she paid no attention.

No doubt sensing this as an opportunity to escape him, she wriggled, squirmed and twisted until he feared she would hurt herself. However, her strength was no match for his and he had no fear of her shouting out.

Yet, with her bottom brushing his crotch, his body responded of its own accord, creating a storm of sensation he would have preferred not to suffer. As he held Kendall for several long minutes, sweat broke out on his forehead. His pulse sped at her proximity. The men in the chopper seemed to take an eternity to move on with their search, and as he breathed in the earthy scent of mud, rain and a light citrus scent from her hair, it became increasingly difficult to pretend Kendall wasn't a very desirable woman.

Last night, as he'd gone over contingency plans, he hadn't anticipated this kind of reaction. But then, he hadn't considered he'd have to hold her this closely, or that the top of her head seemed made to fit under his chin. Or that her slick skin would be so soft. Or her conversation would be so impertinent, intriguing and intelligent.

Since Kendall's father was eccentric and brilliant, Web should have taken into account that his daughter might have inherited his intellect. But Web had gone into the mission with a prejudice about her that had come from reading a too-brief file. Because she'd always lived in a small town, because she'd dropped out of college to nurse her dying mother, because she was willing to marry a man she'd known for less than six months, he'd expected Kendall to be more naive, less suspicious of him. So now he found himself unprepared to deal with his attraction to her on a variety of levels, both physical and mental.

"Mmm." She tried screaming through his hand.

Web's friends would have found his situation comical. He didn't, though. Nor did he think it ironic that the first woman he'd been attracted to in a long time believed he might kill her. The soft sounds escaping from her sealed lips wouldn't carry far, but they needed to keep moving. And walking with his hand clamped over her mouth wasn't a viable option.

He tried reasoning with her. "My choices are to knock you out and carry you, or you can cooperate. What's it going to be?"

"Uh. Mm."

"I'll take that to mean you'll cooperate. Since you've proved that I can't trust you, I'm going to gag you. Sorry." From his pocket, Web removed a relatively clean piece of material that he'd saved from her dress in case a situation such as this one arose, twisted it and slipped it between her teeth. After tying it tightly at the back of her head, he turned her around to face him. "I know it's uncomfortable. But don't touch the gag, and I won't tie your hands. Once we're out of shouting range, you can remove the gag. Okay?"

She nodded, her eyes firing angry missiles, even as she blinked back tears.

"I'm not going to hurt you." Even as he said the words, he knew she didn't believe him. With every muscle taut with anger, she held her shoulders stiff, her back straight, her neck taut. Resigned to her hostility, he pointed. "We'll head north. You set the pace."

They walked for fifteen minutes, going through several fast-running streams, around thick underbrush of mountain laurel, sumac, azaleas and rhododendron and around the edges of a low-lying area of cypress. At least the rain would cleanse the air of their scent and the ground water would confuse any dogs set on their trail. As a snake slithered through the grass, he set his feet down with care. A crow cawed, and rabbits darted. Meanwhile, he racked his brain, trying to think of anything he could say to convince her that he wasn't about to murder her. But he came up with zip.

The storm finally slowed to a drizzle and then stopped, but the trees continued to drip and the humidity prevented their clothes from drying. He stopped in a rocky area. "Okay. You can remove the gag."

Her hands had trouble with the knot, so he untied it for her. He half expected a diatribe of curses to follow, but she breathed deeply and didn't say a word. He hadn't a clue what she was thinking, but he shouldn't have cared. His thoughts should have been focused on covering their trail, on figuring out what to do next. He kept wanting to reassure her, but didn't know how.

"Do you need to rest?"

"I'm okay."

"How're your feet holding up?"

"I'm okay," she repeated, but she wasn't.

Now that they'd stopped, he could see her shivering and clenching her jaw to keep her teeth from chattering. He wished he could warm her with his body heat, but even in the moonlight he could see her outrage. The last thing she'd welcome was his touch. He could stop and build a fire but suspected they couldn't afford to waste that kind of time. "Look, I don't know who sabotaged the chopper, but whoever it was may be on our tail."

She spoke carefully, as if afraid he might strike her if she said the wrong thing. "Maybe the chopper going down was an accident. Maybe no one is after us except good people who are attempting a rescue.

Maybe you haven't thought out all the consequences of your actions.''

"Maybe."

"But you don't agree?"

"In my business, I've survived by assuming the worst. By being careful. My boss, Kincaid, is a fanatic when it comes to maintaining equipment. He hires only the best men and mechanics. It's much more likely that Franklin got wind of our attempt to protect you and tried to stop us."

"But according to your theory, Franklin wanted to use me. He didn't want me dead. And you never did say how my father is connected to Franklin," she prodded.

"We aren't sure of all the details." He started walking along a deer path, and she kept up with him where the path was wide, fell back behind him when the trail narrowed to allow only single file.

"What do you mean, you aren't sure?" Her voice rose in bitter annoyance mixed with a saucy Southern drawl. "Are you saying you made me miss my own wedding on a hunch?"

"Before Franklin was transferred to Alabama, he was one of the men assigned to protect your father. The two of them became friends."

"So now you're saying both my father and my fiancé are traitors?"

"No." He winced at her razor-sharp tone. "I'm saying that Franklin cozied up to your father to learn his weakness."

"His weakness?" She sighed. "Look, I'm wet, tired and cold. You have to explain better because I'm certainly not following your line of reasoning— assuming you have one."

He ignored her sarcasm, knowing it was due to discomfort and frustration. "Your father's weakness is you."

"Ha," she snorted. "Now I know you're making up fairy tales. I've never spoken to my father. Never received so much as a birthday card."

Web slapped himself on the forehead and stopped dead in his tracks. She almost bumped into him. After reaching into his pocket, he removed a photograph. "Dr. Davis may not have ever spoken to you, but he loved you."

"Right. And next you're going to tell me that I've won the lottery."

He handed her the picture and shined his penlight on it. "Look."

She scowled at the gray-haired scientist and, front and center on Dr. Davis's desk, the picture of her, wearing her high school graduation cap and gown. He pointed out a detail she might have otherwise missed. "In the corner of your picture is another snapshot of you when you were five." When she remained silent, Web continued, "You do recognize your father?"

"My mom had a wedding picture of the two of them. He's older here. But yes, it's him." She swallowed hard. "But I don't understand. How did he get these pictures of me?"

"I don't know. But obviously, he kept track of you over the years. In his own way he loves you."

"If he'd loved me he would have found a way to stay around and do his research."

"His work was dangerous. Maybe he didn't wish to put you in danger. But whatever his reasons, he loved you, and Franklin knew it. We think Franklin intended to take you out of the country in order to blackmail your father into doing what he wanted.''

Her eyes snapped up from the picture to stare at him. ''What Franklin wanted?''

''Right now your father is voluntarily stashed in a secret location. Franklin's scheme was to use you to prevent your father from completing his work.''

''Use me? How?''

''We don't have all the details. Just enough to know Franklin meant you harm and that you need protection.''

Along with a strong measure of disbelief, the sass was back in her tone. ''And you expect me to actually trust you based on the meager evidence of a picture, which any computer nerd could have altered in PhotoShop?''

''I have other evidence.'' Web pulled out the tiny camcorder from his pocket and held it up. ''We caught Franklin on video.''

''You were watching him? Why?''

''The details are classified. But his movements made one of our agents suspicious.''

''Show me,'' she demanded.

''I planned to, but I'm not sure how much juice is left in the battery. We may need what's left for more important things.''

Suspicion flared in her eyes. ''Like what?''

''Our survival.''

KENDALL TRUDGED BEHIND WEB, her thoughts a mass of confusion, her feet aching. If there was real evidence on that camcorder she wanted to see it, but Web seemed determined to save the batteries so he could start a fire, and she didn't know whether to believe him or not. Web's story seemed concocted out of a nightmare. And while she'd always wanted to believe that the father who'd disappeared had cared for her, hearing about him now seemed too much like a story contrived to tell her exactly what she wanted to hear.

What fatherless child didn't dream that someday their dad would return, sweep them into their arms and vow their love? Kendall knew life was made up of the good, the bad and the nuances between. Just because she'd wished to meet her father for her entire childhood didn't mean the fantasy had much chance of coming true.

And yet she couldn't dismiss what Web had told her when so many facts fit what she knew to be correct. According to her mother, her father had been brilliant and eccentric with a deep interest in engines and motors and fuel-cell cars. Apparently her fanatical, inventor father had always been obsessed in creating the ultimate green machine. Her mother had said he'd vowed to make some kind of engine system that ran on hydrogen and oxygen and spouted off heat and water vapor as by-products. Give him twenty years, funding and peace and quiet and he would change the balance of power in a world no longer dependent on Middle Eastern fuel. Kendall had always believed her father had used science as his excuse to avoid family responsibility, and it irked her that Web now claimed that her father was so important that he was once again ruining her life.

Christopher Davis had contributed only one thing to her life—his seed. He hadn't helped financially or emotionally. And if he'd somehow kept track of Kendall through the years, then he'd known about her mother's death. Yet had he come to the funeral? Had he phoned? Sent a card? No.

A burst of anger at him flared then burned inward. She shouldn't care about a man so egocentric as her father. She didn't like having feelings for him at all. Recently she'd strived for indifference, and she'd thought she'd actually succeeded—until now. Web's story fit all too well into the facts she had about her dad.

And Franklin was in the FBI. His marriage proposal had seemed to come out of the blue. Although Franklin had offered her his friendship, their relationship lacked the kind of passion she'd always hoped for. But she'd attributed the lack to her state of grief over losing her mother. But what about Franklin's passion for her? He'd never seemed to notice how she'd looked, even when she'd taken care with her appearance. He'd never once tried to push for a physical relationship beyond a few kisses. But were those the actions of a man who was in love?

In addition, Web's explanation had her questioning how much she didn't know about Franklin. She'd assumed he hadn't introduced her to co-workers and friends because he'd been new to the area. He'd claimed not to have any family. And she'd believed him when he'd said they'd have to make their own. At the time, she'd seen no reason for him to lie.

Oh, Franklin had given her reasons for his actions, telling her that he moved so often that he preferred to rent fully furnished properties and took few personal possessions with him. A loner, he'd concentrated a lot of attention on her. She'd been flattered and needy after the death of her mother, soaking up his kindness without questioning his story. And now she wondered how much she really loved him, especially if a complete stranger like Web could make her doubt Franklin's motives.

She wanted to see Web's video proof.

Between the expense of taking her by helicopter, the picture of her father and her growing assurance that Web didn't intend to murder or rape her, her uncertainty about Franklin was growing. Was her honeymoon an excuse for Franklin to take her out of the country to blackmail her father into stopping his work as Web claimed? Was Web really trying to hide her from terrorists to protect her?

Web seemed too rock solid, too in control, too sympathetic and sincere to be a liar. She'd noted his erection when he'd held her and had been immensely relieved when he'd ignored his condition. Perhaps Web even believed that he was protecting her, but that didn't mean his boss, Kincaid, was on the up-and-up.

Wishing she had more information to go on than her impressions of Web, wishing he wasn't so determined to save his batteries and that he'd show her his video evidence, she focused on the facts. Web hadn't hurt her. In fact, since he'd kidnapped her, he'd gone out of his way to make her more comfortable. She would never forget his hand holding hers during that wild helicopter landing. Or how the big man had altered her dress and shoes. Or how after she'd tried to scream for help, he'd gagged her but had left her hands free.

While she didn't necessarily believe his wild story, she no longer believed he meant her harm. If he'd wanted to kill her she'd be dead by now. Yet, if Franklin could fool her, then so could Web, who could be lying through his straight, white, charming teeth. After they reached civilization, he could be the one who tried to use his hold on her against her father, not some mysterious saboteur.

"So what's your plan for me?" she asked, breaking the silence of their march as much to distract herself from her disturbing thoughts and her wet clothes as to find out some answers.

"To keep you safe from terrorists until we either deal with Franklin or your father finishes his invention."

Her father had been working on his invention since before she'd been born, twenty-four years ago. "And how long will that be?"

"We're uncertain."

Frustration escalating, she tried again. "Where are you taking me?"

"We had a safe house set up in Mobile. However, now that my cover may be blown, we'll have to make other arrangements. First we need to get out of this forest." He stopped abruptly at the edge of a lake.

Surrounded by trees, the lake looked so peaceful under the moonlit sky that had cleared of clouds now that the rain had stopped. But no welcoming house lights shone on the water. No cars rushed by. For that matter, she saw no sign of a road.

"Why don't you rest and I'll scrounge us up some dinner," he suggested as if he could order takeout and have it delivered.

Thankful to take the weight off her aching feet, she settled on a flat spot atop a rock. When Web

took a scrap of her abandoned crinoline out of his
sleeve, she shook her head in surprise. She'd had no
idea he'd found and saved the item. He removed his
knife and hacked away at the material, and she
watched in weary fascination. In no time, he'd separated the netting from the lining, woven the netting
around a branch and headed out knee-deep into the
lake to fish.

If she planned another escape, this would be a
good moment to try. But a hundred-yard head start
wasn't enough. He'd overtake her within minutes.
She'd be prudent to wait for a better chance when
he took her back to civilization—especially since she
no longer believed he meant to hurt her. And if she
hung around, she might learn more about her father.
Besides, she had no doubt Web would catch their
dinner, and food would fill her hollow stomach.

This morning she'd been too nervous to eat and
then she'd skipped lunch as she'd showered and
dressed for her wedding. Between the hairdresser
and fixing her makeup, she'd found herself rushing,
with no time to eat. After at least an hour of walking,
she'd used up lots of calories and she'd already
learned that Web did what he said. She hoped he
didn't expect her to eat the fish raw. Sushi might be
chic, but she preferred her food cooked, thank you
very much.

Under the moonlight Web stood so still that the
water ceased to ripple around him. He remained
there for so long that the birds they'd scared away
returned, along with the chirping crickets and croak-
ing frogs.

When he finally moved, he did so with a grace
that suggested he'd performed the action many times

before. Scooping and tossing the netting and fish high onto the bank, knowing his beached catch couldn't escape. Some men would gloat but Web squatted, untangled the fish from the netting and headed back into the lake. "If you can gather some wood, I'll make a fire after I catch another bass."

And then you'll show me the video?" she asked. Although relieved he intended to cook the fish, pleased about the thought of a fire that would dry out their clothes and keep back wild animals, she needed to see the video.

He nodded. "One thing at a time. First I'll start the fire, then we'll see what we have left in the battery. The trick's going to be igniting this fuel-soaked slip that I stripped from the netting and to find some dry kindling."

Her hopes rose. She wanted an end to the uncertainty of whether she could trust Web. "Nothing is dry."

"I'll peel off some bark and dig out dry wood underneath. Should do the trick."

She restrained a smile of admiration. "You should have tried out for *Survivor*."

"I wouldn't last past the first or second round."

"Why's that?" she asked, curious how he saw himself.

He shot her a wolfish smile. "The strong ones always get voted off by the weaker ones."

"True." However, if she had to be stranded in the woods, she was glad it was with someone who knew how to find dinner. And *strong* described him perfectly. He possessed a self-confidence that made her feel comfortable in a way that Franklin never had.

"While I look for the firewood, I'm going to make a pit stop. It might take a few minutes to untie—"

"I understand. You'll have all the privacy you need."

If she intended to run, now would be the perfect time—except then she might never get to see the video. While she might get a fifteen-minute head start before he followed, that wouldn't be enough. However, she had no intention of running blindly into the woods when he would show her his proof of Franklin's perfidy if she stayed. Was she letting her hungry belly and the potential comfort of fire dictate her actions? Or was she simply beginning to trust Web? She didn't know. But when she weighed which she'd prefer, heading alone into the dark woods or staying with Web, she found that making the decision was easier than she'd anticipated, or perhaps easier than it should have been. But she didn't think she could develop Stockholm Syndrome in less that twenty-four hours and went about her business of seeing to her personal needs and collecting firewood.

She returned to find that he'd cleaned and filleted the fish and had them speared, ready to cook. She dumped the firewood in a pile beside him, careful not to disturb the tiny fire he'd kindled and was carefully feeding.

He didn't take his eyes from the fire as he burned dollar bills to encourage tiny sticks to light. "I wasn't sure you'd come back."

She snapped branches into smaller pieces. "I'm still not sure that I made the right choice."

"Are we ever?" He blew lightly on the fire. The

flames danced in his eyes and she caught sight of a slight smile on a face that no longer looked so stern.

"Well, with that kind of encouragement, now I feel so much better." She didn't know what about Web caused her sarcasm to come out, especially when she knew how much her peculiar sense of humor irritated most men. She'd had to curb her tongue around Franklin who told her in no uncertain terms that he preferred a gentler attitude, but Web seemed amused by her comments. Although Kendall had missed growing up without a father, she'd never learned how to suppress her natural curiosity, intelligence or wit on the rare occasions men were around.

Web fed increasingly larger branches into the fire. "Personally, I'll feel better after we eat. I'm starved." When the flames brightened and the wood popped and snapped, he arranged the speared fish over the flames. "If you'll turn these often, I'll see about finding us water to drink."

She was glad he hadn't suggested drinking from the lake when they had no idea if it was contaminated and would make them sick. Without a pot or cup, they couldn't even boil it. While she tended the fish, feeling like some stone-age cave woman squatting by the fire, Web returned with several long-stalked plants.

"These are all for you. I've already drunk." He gestured for her to stand, sliced the stalk open with his knife and tipped the stalk to her mouth.

Clean, sweet water dribbled, then gushed into her mouth. She swallowed quickly, ignoring the overflow down her chin. With all the rain, she hadn't realized how thirsty she'd been until the cool liquid slid down her parched throat. "Thanks."

"Let me know when you want more." He leaned toward the fire and examined the fish. "Looks done."

While he'd been gone, she'd ripped two large leaves from nearby plants. "I thought these would work as plates."

"Good idea." Web placed the fish on the leaves. "We should probably let the meat cool to avoid burning our fingers, but I've never been able to wait that long." He broke off a piece, then sucked in his breath and fanned his fingers to cool them.

"You've done this often?"

"My dad took my brothers and me camping in the wilds of Colorado almost every weekend, rain or shine, winter or summer."

No wonder he was so comfortable in the woods. "Your mom didn't go?"

"She died after I was born."

"Sorry." She broke off a tiny slice of fish, but it was still too hot to eat. "Your father never remarried?"

He shook his head. "It was probably our fault. Not many women wanted to take on three wild hooligans and a mountain man."

She could tell from his tone that the memories were pleasant and she squashed her jealousy. She'd always longed for a brother or sister. "Does your father still live in Colorado?"

"Along with both of my brothers."

"Are they married?"

"Kevin's tried it and divorced twice. Clark is too

busy getting rich to have time for a wife. He claims that all women like to do is shop and spend money.''

''And what about you?'' she asked.

''I'm not the marrying type.''

''Neither was my father.'' The words popped out before she realized how bitter she sounded. She attempted to lighten her tone. ''Oh, he married my mother but after she became pregnant he didn't stick around to give us more than his last name.''

He used his knife to cut the fish into smaller sections that quickly cooled. She popped a piece into her mouth and couldn't believe how great it tasted without any seasoning. ''This is good.''

''Cooking over an open fire always increases the appetite.''

She had no idea if his double entendre was deliberate or accidental but his statement made her uncomfortable. Franklin was sexless compared to Web, but Franklin had also made her feel safe—which made Web's assertion that the man wanted to turn her over to terrorists difficult to believe. They polished off the fish in a tense silence. When they'd finished the last morsels, he tossed the leaves into the lake, rinsed his hands and began to walk back toward the fire.

She glanced at the camcorder battery, prayed there was enough power left.

''Can we try the battery now, please?''

She half expected him to refuse. But instead he placed the battery into the casing and flipped on the power. He fast-forwarded to the position he wanted, then handed her the video. ''Press the button on the right.''

Her mouth went dry and her hand shook. Now

that the moment was here, she wasn't sure she wanted to know. Either her fiancé was plotting against her with terrorists, or she was in the middle of nowhere with a madman. But she had to know. Pressing down the button, she saw Franklin's face, heard him speaking clearly on his phone. "The bitch agreed to marry me," Franklin sneered. "I'll deliver her next week in Cairo as we agreed." Franklin paused, then laughed. "Don't worry. She doesn't suspect a thing."

"Oh…God." Her hands shook so badly she couldn't hold the camera. Despite everything Web had told her, Franklin's betrayal shocked her to her core. Although Web had explained the details, she hadn't really believed him until now.

"You okay?"

Shock had numbed her and her voice cracked. "Could I have another drink, please?"

"Sure."

Before Web had risen to his feet, the silence of the forest shattered.

A rifle shot blasted through the night.

Chapter Four

Kendall's brain had barely registered Franklin's betrayal as several shots kicked up the mud between her and Web, indicating striking bullets, and Web lunged at her. Knocking her over, he covered her with his bulky body. At the same time he tossed handfuls of dirt into the fire, dousing them in darkness.

With her face pushed into the dirt, the wet grass resoaking her dress, which had only begun to dry, she was all too cognizant of her surroundings. If she was supposed to die, her life should have flashed before her, but instead, she became aware of too many details. Her heart pounded so hard that the blood rushed to her head. Moist dirt on her lips tasted like blood, but her lips didn't sting, although her ribs ached. She shook with the damp icy cold of panic—except where Web pressed against her. His warm breath fanned her ear and neck. His chest warmed her back.

Web's first rush to topple her had almost knocked the wind out of her, but he'd quickly taken the bulk of his weight off her, even as he kept his body between her and harm. She found it ironic that in the few hours she'd known him, his large bulk had gone from frightening her to protecting her.

The shooting stopped as suddenly as it had begun, leaving her stunned at the unnatural stillness, yet wary. Frogs no longer croaked. Birds didn't caw. Nocturnal animals held their collective breaths as if an evil aura engulfed them. Even the wind had ceased to blow.

Web smoothly rolled from her. "Kendall, we need to get out of here."

"Duh." Shaking, her stomach rolling, she began to shove to her feet.

He tugged her back down. "Crawl. The shooter might have a nightscope. And despite being caked in mud, your dress is still white enough to draw attention. Let's make shooting us as difficult for him as possible."

Nightscope? Shooter? She swallowed back the crazy urge to break into hysterical laughter. Until the last twelve hours, Kendall's life had been relatively uneventful. Her idea of a big night was dinner and a movie. Her only run-in with the law was a speeding ticket a month after she'd gotten her driver's license. She didn't even know any criminals, and now someone was shooting at her.

Probably the only reason she was still alive was because of Web's fast thinking. And her own commonsense decision to stay with him. If earlier she'd taken off alone, she might now be dead.

Fighting back the panicky giggle spiraling up her throat, she crawled in the direction Web pointed, ignoring the mud, the slime, the sucking, slithering muck and the mosquitoes feasting on her tender flesh. She crawled, putting one hand in front of the other, one knee down, then the other. Knowing that Web was right behind, his nose inches from her bottom, was the least of her concerns.

"Who was shooting at us?" she whispered, swatting uselessly at the bugs.

"Scoop up some mud and slather it over you like suntan lotion. It'll protect you."

"Ugh," she complained.

"Pretend it's that expensive mud from the Dead Sea that goes for fifty bucks an ounce," he teased.

Tentatively, she followed his suggestion. Immediate relief from the itching bug bites had her glopping more muck over her neck, forehead and face as well as her arms. "If Franklin could see me now, he'd freak."

"The question is not if he'd freak, but if he'd shoot you." Web's tone was soft, grim, reminding her that although she'd seen the evidence that Franklin was not who he seemed, his treachery had yet to really sink into her brain.

"I suppose you're going to say 'I told you so,' but really, Web, I'm having trouble buying the idea that Franklin is now trying to kill me. If I'm dead he can't turn me over to terrorists."

"True. But someone shot at us back there. And if it's Franklin, he's desperate to cover up his plans." He added, "We can stand up now."

"How do you know it's safe?"

"I don't. But we can't crawl all night. And if the shooter had a nightscope, he probably would have taken more shots by now."

Standing was more effort than she'd have liked. Her knees and shoulders ached, but stretching upright took a few kinks out of her neck. Exasperation chased away some of her fear. Although the video had gone a long way toward convincing her of Franklin's guilt, she wondered if the sound could have been dubbed. Sure, she'd heard Franklin's voice, but with just a few word changes, he could have really said something innocent and been made to appear guilty. Still that was an awful lot of trouble for someone to go to just to convince her Franklin was guilty. "We don't know the shooter is Franklin. Or if it is him, perhaps he was shooting at you because he believes that I'm in danger," she countered, wondering how her brain could function and her voice could sound so impudent when she was shaking inside and out.

"We aren't going back to find out." Web headed away from the lake, taking a new direction as if he had an internal compass and knew exactly where he was going.

"I would have thought a military type like you would set a trap to catch the hunter."

"If I was alone, I might do that." Annoyance and amusement vied for supremacy in his tone. "But my mission isn't to nab or identify the shooter, but to keep you safe."

She recalled Web risking his life to protect her with his body, like some kind of heroic Secret Service agent, and her normal sarcasm dwindled into the night. Web believed in his mission and was willing to pay the price with his life. Kendall knew plenty of people with strong convictions, but Web backed up the talk with forthright, undeniable action that convinced her more than anything he might say that he was one of the good guys.

Despite the video, she still had trouble believing

that Franklin was working with terrorists. She watched television and read the newspaper. She understood how interdepartmental agencies squabbled and stepped on one another's turf. Since 9/11 the feuding had supposedly stopped and the various law enforcement agencies had pulled together, but human nature meant that people trusted those they worked with day in and day out and kept strangers out of the loop. For all she knew, Franklin's file could have been mixed up with another agent's, the video could be faked. He could be a total innocent. And yet…was she refusing to believe the evidence that Web had put right before her eyes because she couldn't face the truth of Franklin's duplicity? After seeing Web operate, if the other men in his unit were the same caliber as he'd claimed, she'd bet they didn't make many mistakes.

With the walk long and arduous, she had too much to think about. The night wasn't particularly cold, but between the breeze and her wet clothing, she welcomed the brisk pace Web set that upped her circulation and stopped her shivering. Deep in thought, she failed to watch her step and tripped.

Web reached out to steady her. His hand on her arm felt good. Too good. She jerked back, wondering what was wrong with her. After all she'd been through, the last thing she should be doing was appreciating another man's touch.

"I'm sorry to push you so hard." Web's comforting voice only served to make her feel guiltier.

"It's not your fault someone decided to shoot at us." She sighed. "You don't suppose some hunter mistook us for a deer?"

"Not with us silhouetted by the fire."

She glanced back over her shoulder, wondering if the shooter was about to open fire on them again. She saw nothing but the darkness of the forest, lurking shadows and the occasional firefly's tiny flare. The sudden baying of dogs caused an icicle of fear to stab down her spine. "You think the shooter has dogs?"

"I doubt it. More likely the Forest Service called local law enforcement. Luckily for us, most dogs are trained to track scent over the ground."

"Most?" she asked, sure he would have an informative answer.

He didn't disappoint her. "Some rescue dogs track scent through the air. Either way the rain should keep them off our trail. If we don't find a road by daylight, we'll find a spot to hole up to avoid being seen and to conserve fluids. Right now it's cool, but with the sun rising, dehydration can become a factor."

The man was a fountain of knowledge, but she had to bite back a groan at the idea of walking all night. It was probably only midnight and already exhaustion was starting to make her head droop.

"I'm not sure I can walk all night."

"Okay."

She'd expected him to nag her, shame her or encourage her. Instead he tucked the information away as if he accepted her word that she'd almost reached the limits of her physical strength. "I can go another hour, maybe two," she guessed.

"While it was still light, I noted a break in the trees on that ridge. It might be a fire break, but I'm hoping for a road."

"Don't get your hopes too high," she warned

him. "Some of these back roads can wind for miles through the forest without a gas station or even a car passing by." Even as she warned him, she wondered what she'd do if they reached civilization. After the shooting, after seeing the video, she no longer knew if attempting to run from Web was a good idea. More and more, she believed Franklin's guilt. Too tired to decide for certain, she put off making a decision.

SENSING IF HE PUSHED the pace she might collapse, Web had slowed their tempo to no more than a three-mile-per-hour stroll. With her walking in front, he used the extra time to cover their trail and once or twice laid a false one. She'd walked for four hours longer than she'd told him she could. But two hours ago, in exhaustion, Kendall had stopped talking. She needed rest. Water. Food and a hot shower.

When he suspected she couldn't go on, he stopped, removed the protein bar he'd saved for this moment and unwrapped it, then handed it to her. "Eat."

She took a bite, chewed slowly and tried to hand it back to him.

He shook his head. "You finish it."

"No. We share," she insisted, so tired she could barely speak.

While he appreciated the sentiment, she required the carbs way more than he did. "My body is used to deprivation. Yours isn't. Eat."

"But—"

"Don't waste energy arguing. I could go for at least three days before I'm as exhausted as you are right now. But if I have to carry you, it'll be that much harder on me.''

"Okay.'' She ate slowly and had difficulty swallowing. "Do we have any more water?''

They'd been gradually heading uphill. "The stalks don't grow around here.''

With the first signs of dawn approaching on the eastern horizon, he knew they needed to hide. But thoughts of her going without food or water for another twelve hours made him wince. Perhaps he could find a place for her to wait and he could scour the area for supplies. But he didn't want to leave her alone and unprotected. First, she was too tired to think clearly, and second, he hadn't forgotten the shooter that might or might not still be on their trail.

"Stop.'' Ahead of him, she sank to her knees. At first he thought she'd simply keeled over. But then he saw her plucking juicy blackberries from a briar patch. She popped one into her mouth, then handed him a fat few berries. "Go on. There's lots of them.''

Those berries, sweet and juicy, tasted like nectar from the gods. He'd been so focused on covering their trail he might not have spotted them, and that she had made him appreciate her all the more. In the military, Web had been through survival training and knew that people who panicked often got themselves killed. But as unaccustomed as Kendall was to walking long distances with no sleep and little food or water, she had kept her head.

They plucked all the berries they could reach and ate them as they walked. "If my navigating is on target, that ridge should be in sight soon.''

"And then what?''

"We find some transportation."

"As filthy as we are, no one is going to pick us up looking like this."

"Let me worry about that."

"Web?"

"Yeah."

"You aren't going to hurt anybody, are you?"

"Now, do I strike you as a violent person?"

"Those calluses on your right hand, particularly the one between your thumb and pointer finger indicate you've done more than your share of shooting."

"I'm not carrying a weapon."

"Your knuckles are flat. Doesn't that happen from punching a bag?"

"A *makiwara.*"

"A what?"

"It's a stick with padding on the end. Martial arts people prefer it to a nice, soft bag. But let me ease your mind. Right now I'm thinking about hot showers, clean clothing and a breakfast of eggs, English muffins, bacon. A gallon of orange juice and—"

"Grits?"

"Yuck. I'd rather eat C-rations."

"So if you don't intend to conk anyone on the head to get us transportation, exactly how do you intend to—"

"There. It is a road." He took her hand and helped her the last few meters. But when she would have walked into the open, he held her back. As she'd predicted, the road was empty of traffic, but he hoped as the night faded away into day, they'd come across a few travelers. In the meantime, they really needed to wash and he heard the enticing sound of gurgling water.

With a stunned expression, Kendall's eyes narrowed. "Have I finally lost my mind?"

He chuckled. "Why?"

"Am I imagining the sound of running water?"

KENDALL DIDN'T HESITATE to wash in the stream while Web stood guard. After reviewing Web's story and what she knew about Franklin practically all night, she was about ninety percent certain Web was there to protect her. While the idea of Franklin marrying her, then turning her over to terrorists to blackmail her father into stopping his work still seemed far-fetched, Web had offered her too many facts that fit together for her not to realize he was probably telling her the truth.

Her shock had given way to anger that Franklin would betray her, her father and the country. Her fury had given her the energy to keep walking for far longer than she might have otherwise. But even in her exhaustion, she realized she should have been more hurt by Franklin's betrayal. Perhaps it was simply too much to sort out at once.

However, a few things were clear. By now she understood that Web had too much honor to take so much as an illicit peek while she bathed. Oh, he might tease, his eyes might burn hotly, but he wasn't the type to do anything but go directly after what he wanted. Sneaking was so beneath him that she wasn't the least bit worried about her privacy. Especially after Web led her to a secluded spot surrounded by greenery where the water gurgled over rocks and pooled into a bathing area with a gently sloped bank.

Comfortable enough to remove her battered dress and underwear, Kendall ducked the material underwater and scrubbed as much of the dirt out as possible. Then she wrung the excess moisture from the satin that would never again be a pristine white. She didn't bother spreading it over a bush to dry. Her bath had to be quick—she couldn't forget that the sniper might still be out there. Dipping her head under the clean water, she held her breath and let the cool temperature wash away the sting of insect bites and the itching of dried mud. With her palms, she quickly scrubbed her neck, shoulders, and the parts of her back that she could reach. Although she would have appreciated a bar of soap, shampoo and clean, dry clothes to change into, the refreshing bath was so sweet it washed away much of her exhaustion.

Web had told her he'd scout out their perimeter, but he would remain within shouting distance if she needed him. So while she didn't splash or float, she let her mind drift as her body rejuvenated. And she allowed herself a moment to close her eyes and enjoy the blissful peace of the moment.

She didn't think about yesterday or tomorrow. Perhaps the hardships and shock she'd suffered made the moment perfect. She was happy to be alive, and for now that was enough. She emerged and leaned against a rock to let the sun caress her skin, but didn't wait for the warmth to dry her since she had to don her wet underwear and dress. However, in the warm morning, she wouldn't take long to dry. She ran her fingers through her hair to comb it, ready to face whatever the day and Web had to offer.

"I'm all done," she called out. "Your turn."

He emerged from the forest, his hair damp, his eyelashes spiked with a few stray water droplets. He'd washed his clothing but, still wet, with only a few dry patches, his jeans and shirt clung to him outlining his muscular body. "There was another pool downstream." His eyes gleamed mischievously. "And I've found us a ride…of sorts."

"Of sorts?"

"Thanks to the tropical storm that blew through here last week, a brush crew is out clearing the hiking trails of downed trees. We should hear the chainsaws gearing up any minute."

"What does that have to do with our ride?"

"I borrowed the crew's pickup truck." He led her away from the creek in a new direction to where he'd parked a green truck with the Forest Service's yellow emblem emblazoned on the side. "Don't worry, we aren't stranding them in the wilderness. They have radios and cell phones."

She hesitated, staring at the truck. "I've never stolen anything before."

He gestured her toward the truck. "Have you ever been shot at before?"

"You had to remind me?" she muttered.

"Besides, we'll return the vehicle. In fact, the bright-green color makes us way too conspicuous to drive into town. We'll have to ditch it and find alternate transportation."

"Okay."

She climbed into the truck, opened the glove compartment and searched for a map as Web started the engine and drove down the road. Disappointed when she didn't turn up so much as a scrap of paper, she flicked on the radio and tuned in to the local station. After hearing the tail end of Toby Keith's "Country of the Red, White and Blue," the local news came on. The radio DJ began to talk about Canfield's own runaway bride who'd left her groom at the altar and hadn't been heard from since.

"He's talking about me."

She imagined Franklin's humiliation. Standing at the church in his tux, waiting for her, and then when she didn't arrive, his having to make excuses to her friends and his associates. Hell, she didn't feel sorry for him—not since he was the one who planned to turn her over to terrorists.

Kendall was about to flip off the station when the DJ continued, "If anyone has information on the whereabouts of Kendall Davis, a five-foot-five-inch blonde with green eyes, please contact the sheriff's department immediately." The DJ went on to other news about a helicopter crash and the search-and-rescue mission currently going on in the forest before finishing up with the weather and the last night's high school football score.

"Oh, God." She dropped her face into her hands. She'd been concentrating so hard on survival that until now she hadn't realized all the ramifications of her disappearance. Her best friend, Beth, would be frantic.

Web's take was very different from hers. "The news is good. So far the authorities haven't connected your disappearance to the helicopter going down."

She stared at him. By now she shouldn't be

shocked at the cool, rational way he thought through the situation. But right at the moment she was more concerned about reassuring her friend than about what local law enforcement might know. "When we get to town, I have to make a phone call."

"And call whom? And say what?"

"I have people who care about me. I have to let them know I'm all right."

Web shook his head, a lock of black hair dropping over one eye. "I'm sorry, but that's not a good idea. Whoever tried to shoot us last night may be watching your friends. Showing up or calling them could not only get you killed but also endanger them. Not knowing what happened to you may be emotionally upsetting, but it won't kill them."

"That's...harsh."

Clearly irritated by her comment, he shoved the stray lock off his forehead. "I trying to do what's best."

She glared at him. "Yeah, right."

"My number-one priority is to get you into less conspicuous clothes, check in with my boss, then head out of town to a safe place."

"Oh, so it's okay for you to let your boss know we survived, but I can't tell Beth."

"We're operating on a need-to-know basis."

"Beth is a very good friend. She's not going to take my disappearance lying down." Beth and Kendall had been best friends since first grade. Outwardly, they didn't seem to have much in common. Beth was tall, dark-haired, dark-eyed and curvy. Her parents had money and had put in a swimming pool during their sophomore year of high school where they'd had some fine parties. Beth was a fireball of energy and a loyal friend. She'd always known she wanted to be a newscaster and she went about achieving that in a straightforward fashion. After attaining her journalism degree, she had her daddy buy the local television station, assuring her a job. And she loved a good fight. No way would she take Kendall's disappearance without creating a fuss, even if she'd never liked Franklin and hadn't approved of the engagement.

Ever since Web had taken Kendall from the limousine and stopped her marriage to Franklin, Kendall had mostly avoided thinking about him on a personal level. Sure, she'd had brief bursts of anger here and there, but her heart didn't ache for him. And it should have. But she didn't feel that gullible, either.

If Franklin was the double agent Web claimed, her fiancé hadn't just fooled her but the people at the FBI, too. So if he was guilty, he had to be extremely good at what he did. She shouldn't feel stupid for trusting him. After all, how could she have known? How did anyone really know what anyone else was like?

And yet, in the short time she'd known Web, she felt she knew him quite well. If Web's bride hadn't shown for his wedding, she knew Web would have hunted her to the ends of the earth. And he'd tear apart anyone who'd dared harm her.

She glanced over at the man driving the truck. He drove with both hands on he wheel, relaxed yet vigilant. When they finally turned out of the national forest, he acted as though he knew exactly where he was going.

"We need to get off the road before someone spots this truck." Web pulled off the highway and shut down the engine. "I noticed a farmhouse a quarter mile back. Let's hope no one's home."

Chapter Five

With a pickup truck in the driveway, Web suspected someone was home. He figured the isolated farmhouse, where he stood a chance of controlling the situation, was a good place to find out if Kendall was with him or against him. He couldn't be sure if she'd been biding her time, pretending to go along with him, or if she still intended to try to get away.

The shooter and the video clip had to have gone a long way toward helping her see Web's side of things. But he knew too well that people often believed what they wanted to believe despite all the evidence to the contrary. Changing one's mind required admitting one had been wrong—never an easy thing to do. However, Kendall had adapted to her situation much more easily than he'd expected, revealing a resilience that was as much a part of her spirited nature as her keen intelligence.

If Web had been a gambling man, he'd have bet he had a fifty-fifty chance of her sticking by him. But that wasn't good enough. If she still doubted him, he needed to know now, before they returned to civilization. Deliberately, he didn't tell her what to say or do, except that they couldn't make a phone call without endangering the home's occupant. Instead, he'd watch her for signs of what she was really thinking.

Together they walked down the gravel driveway. When a friendly mutt ran out to greet them, Kendall bent and petted the dog, making a new friend by scratching behind his ears.

While the dog distracted her, Web took in the sturdy two-story farmhouse. He noted the front door, the side door and a back deck that could be approached from the woods or serve as a quick getaway route with cover. No telephone wires led from the road to the house. The utilities could be underground or the owners used cell phones as their primary means of communication. As they ambled past the pickup, he spied a key in the ignition. Some of the tension in his shoulders eased. People who thought nothing of leaving their vehicle key around tended to be trusting and honest.

He knocked on the front door and wasn't surprised when an elderly woman opened it without asking who was there. Shoving back a lock of white bangs from bright-blue eyes, her crinkled face broke into a welcoming smile. She glanced from the mutt rubbing against Kendall to her torn bridal dress and beckoned them inside her narrow foyer. "I see you've already met Rascal. Did you folks break down on the road?"

When Kendall remained silent, Web spoke up. "Someone ran us off the road in the park and we got turned around in the woods hiking out."

"You folks come on in. I'm Daisy Arnold."

"Steve and Linda," Web lied, wondering if Kendall would go along.

She passed his first test without hesitation. "Pleased to meet you, ma'am."

Daisy ushered them past a dining room filled with Victorian furniture, vases displaying dried flowers and a spectacular grandfather clock before entering a kitchen with ancient but sparkling appliances. With billowing checkered yellow-and-white curtains, a worn but spotless tablecloth and a crockery jug filled with wildflowers, the atmosphere was warm and homey.

Daisy hefted a glass pitcher. "Would you care for some sweet tea?"

"Thanks." Web placed his arm over Kendall's shoulder. "Is there any chance you might have some clothes we could purchase? I'd hate for Linda's parents to see her like this. They'd think I wasn't taking very good care of my new bride."

Daisy poured them each a glass of sweet tea, then pushed a plate of fresh-cooked biscuits in their direction. "My daughter left some clothes here that might do the trick." She turned to Web. "If you wouldn't mind digging out a chest from a corner of the attic for me...I'll see what I can find. No charge."

Web drained the tea in one long swallow, bit into the best-tasting biscuit of his life and grinned. "My compliments to the chef. Ma'am, this biscuit could compete with any restaurant this side of the Mason-Dixon Line."

"Why, thank you." Daisy beamed at him. "My boys always liked them, too, and could have polished off that entire plate in minutes. There's blackberry preserves and honey over there. Help yourself.

I love to cook, and with the kids all growed up, Mac and me won't finish them before they go stale.''

Kendall sounded sincere. ''Maybe you'd share the recipe? Or is it a family secret?''

''I'd be happy to give you the recipe, but first let's see about those clothes. If they fit, consider them a gift.''

As Web followed Daisy down the hallway and helped her pull steps down from the ceiling that led to the attic, he marveled at Daisy's helpfulness. Small towns in the South had certain advantages if their inhabitants were like Daisy Arnold. She hadn't asked one nosy question about the altered wedding dress. She'd fed them and taken them into her home with a Southern hospitality that made him realize that the cash he'd offered her might be considered an insult. Daisy came from an era where folks helped one another because it was the right thing to do.

He couldn't imagine even one of his neighbors in any of the big cities he'd lived in taking strangers into their home like she'd done for them. This side of life was one Web had rarely seen and it made him feel guilty that he'd lied to the woman about their names.

Daisy climbed up the steps with the agility of a woman half her seventy-plus years. She yanked on a string that hung from the ceiling to turn on a light-bulb. ''There. See that chest under that stuff behind the oval mirror?''

''Yes, ma'am.'' Web dragged the chest out from under an old mattress, assorted cartons filled with books, dishes and old photographs.

Daisy flipped open the lock and he lifted the lid. She dug past an afghan blanket and stacks of sheets, retrieving a pair of worn jeans, a T-shirt that said University of Alabama, a pair of faded red-and-white sneakers and a baseball cap. She handed the clothing over to Kendall with a smile. "You look about my daughter's size while she was in college. After three kids, she'd never fit into these clothes. So they're yours if you want them."

"Thanks. They look perfect." Kendall set aside the cap. "I won't be needing this."

Without the women noticing, Web scooped up the cap and tucked it into his back pocket. He placed the chest back in the corner, turned off the light and hurriedly heaved the steps back into the attic ceiling while Daisy and Kendall went ahead to a bedroom so she could try on the clothes. If Kendall intended to betray him, now would be her best shot.

He stood outside the closed bedroom door, his ear to the wall, ready to barge in and interrupt the conversation if Kendall tried to tell Daisy more than she should or ask to use the phone. He prayed intervention wouldn't be necessary. As the women chatted about the fit of the clothing, he realized that although Kendall hadn't done or said anything suspicious, he still couldn't trust her.

Perhaps she hadn't revealed anything about her situation because she hadn't wanted to upset Daisy. Or perhaps since there was no phone, Kendall was waiting for a better moment. When the two women exited the bedroom and Kendall gave Daisy a piece of note paper, his suspicions skyrocketed.

"Thanks, dear." Daisy patted Kendall's shoulder in a motherly fashion. "Mac adores fried chicken and I can't wait to try out your recipe."

"It's the least I could do in exchange for the clothes."

"They weren't doing anyone any good in that old chest. I'm happy you can use them." Daisy winked at her. "That tight T-shirt does wonders for your figure."

Web had to agree. He hadn't realized Kendall was quite so curvy, but when she'd bathed in that creek, his thoughts had drifted into fantasy where he envisioned water droplets clinging to bare flesh. He'd kept his back to her, but as each tiny coo of pleasure at her bath had reached him, his mind had gone where it had no business going.

He'd imagined her face clean of mud and dirt, her hair clean and silky. Her arms rising to her hair, her breasts tilting upward to the sunlight…and he'd gone off to his own bath, all too aware how attractive he found Kendall when she was covered with mud in a ripped dress. Resisting his desire for her when she'd cleaned up was going to be adding difficulty to an already trying mission.

Although he now found the T-shirt that molded her body a distraction, it was her handwritten note that had his attention. Had she penned a plea for help on the note or a genuine recipe for fried chicken?

KENDALL THOUGHT IT ODD that Web had read her fried chicken recipe. And it wasn't until they'd returned to the road and stuck out their thumbs to hitch that she realized he'd wanted to make sure she hadn't left any secret message with Daisy.

She supposed she couldn't blame him for not trusting her. Especially since she had yet to firmly make up her own mind about her situation. Web had insisted that using the Forest Service's truck again would be too dangerous, and they now stood on the highway shoulder. About to question Web about their next destination, she lost her chance when a dump truck stopped along the road to give them a lift.

Wedged between the burley truck driver and Web, Kendall tried to sort out her thoughts while the two men chatted. This time Web told the driver that they were brother and sister hitching a ride to their mother's funeral. Not only did his tall tale gain them the driver's sympathy but the easy way in which Web lied to cover their tracks told her that the story he'd fed her could also be a lie.

And yet to keep on stubbornly believing that Web wasn't what he said didn't make much sense either, not after she'd seen the video, not after someone else had shot at them. Web wasn't a killer or a rapist. What else could he be but what he'd claimed? She could think of several far-fetched possibilities. He could be a foreign agent trying to use her to get her father to do something. He could be an enemy of Franklin's or possibly be trying to use her to blackmail Franklin.

But that would mean Franklin had lied to her, too. Could her fiancé be much more important than he'd told her?

Think.

How could she verify Web's story? Calling Franklin wouldn't help. If he'd lied to her before, he would simply do so again. She could ask to speak with her father, but she wouldn't recognize his voice. Her thoughts circled. Surely Web had to have some kind of proof, some kind of documentation to verify he was whom he claimed. And yet, what would satisfy her? The word of a police officer that she knew? But she didn't know any police officers.

She was still pondering her dilemma when the dump truck driver stopped in front of Darby's largest shopping center, which consisted of a super discount store, a grocery, a hair salon, a pawn shop and a dry-cleaning establishment. She hopped out, Web thanked the driver again and, after the truck departed, Kendall raised her eyebrow. "Now what?"

"We need toiletries, a change of clothing, wheels and I should check in with my boss. I'm going to ask him to send flowers to Daisy in thanks for her hospitality. Let's find a pay phone."

"I'm surprised you don't have a cell."

"It was in my bag on the chopper. With Jack having direct communication to base, I saw no reason to carry it in my pocket." He gazed at her and guessed, "Yours was left in the limo?"

"Yeah, my departure was too sudden to take all my belongings—which I expect you to replace."

"No problem."

As they headed toward the huge discount store, she rolled her eyes. "My diary was in my bag. I was hoping to record my wedding memories while they were still fresh."

He shot her a charming, don't-make-a-fuss grin. "So, now you'll have plenty of material to start writing a new one."

"Yeah, right."

"This one will be much more exciting," he assured her.

"Why?"

"You'll be writing about me." He chuckled and

placed his arm around her shoulders as they strolled over the hot pavement of the crowded parking lot.

She wasn't sure how she felt about his arm on her shoulder. Was his gesture one of simple affection? She doubted it. Web had dual reasons for everything. He probably wanted them to appear like a couple to any passersby. And maybe he thought she might attempt to make a break for it and his arm would remind her not to try something so foolish.

"I'm not crazy about the idea of some police officer or FBI agent reading my diary," she muttered.

"Shh. Not here, please," he cautioned her as if the teenager unloading the groceries for his mom might be listening or the harried dad with a baby might in actuality be an undercover agent.

His cautious nature that was so much a part of him helped to convince her that he worked undercover for a living. She didn't miss him checking out vehicles as they walked, or his casual steering of her away from a parked van with a snoozing driver behind the wheel, as if a sniper might pop out between the parked cars and start firing. Observant, vigilant, watchful, thoughtful and careful, he always seemed on guard.

She wasn't sure if she felt protected or smothered. But either way, she'd decided not to run. For now. Not with the memory of the shooter in the woods so fresh in her mind. Not after that convincing video.

"Darby isn't that far from Canfield. There's a slim chance we may bump into someone who knows me," she told him.

Web removed the baseball cap from his pocket, placed it on her head and tugged the brim low over her eyes. "If you see anyone you know, try to turn your face away and keep walking."

"And if that doesn't work?"

"We'll play it by ear."

After spotting the phone booths in the front of the store, Web had her go in first, then followed, closing the door behind them. With his bulk blocking her from view, they were safe for now.

He seemed resigned to her hearing at least his end of the conversation. She watched intently as he dialed a ten-digit number, then he covered the mouthpiece while he waited. "Our system connects through five satellites on three continents and is encrypted with the latest classified technology, but it takes a few seconds to go through." He uncovered the mouthpiece. "Logan Kincaid, please."

She was stunned when Web bent and placed the phone low enough for her to hear the entire conversation. And that's when she finally believed Web one hundred percent. He wouldn't permit her to listen in if he wasn't who he claimed.

"Web?"

"Sir, it's me, and Kendall is listening, too. She's not quite sure if she believes that I'm one of the good guys."

"Understood."

"Jack okay?" Web asked about the pilot.

"He made it back in time for Piper to curse him as she gave birth to a healthy, eight-pound, fourteen-ounce boy. I sent champagne, cigars and a bassinet from all of us."

Web grinned. "Great."

"Not so great. We have a problem. Apparently one of Kendall's friends, a Beth Patterson, is a TV anchor for a small station in Canfield. She's causing a ruckus. Kendall's face is everywhere. Newspapers. Television. Posters.''

At Kincaid's words, Kendall's heart warmed. Dear Beth would move heaven and hell to find her. She'd always been the first one to take up a cause, and with her best friend's disappearance, she'd see it as her moral duty to stir up the media.

''Is Beth working with Franklin?'' Web asked.

''They've been in contact. Whether or not they are working together is another matter.''

''We've already left Canfield and someone was on our tail, but I think we've lost him. Can you account for Franklin's whereabouts last night around midnight?''

''He was in Mobile at FBI headquarters.''

''So he wasn't the one shooting at us.'' Kendall breathed out a sigh of relief. While she believed Web, the idea that her fiancé wanted her dead still filled her with horror.

''Just because Franklin didn't do the dirty work himself, doesn't mean he's innocent,'' Kincaid cautioned her.

''What do you suggest, sir?'' Web asked.

''Will Kendall cooperate?''

Web raised an eyebrow and let her speak for herself.

''Yes. Web and you have convinced me that Franklin's not who he claims.''

Web's eyes blazed with approval as he spoke to his boss. ''What would you like us to do?''

''Visit her friend. Tell her a story that will stop the media blitz.''

Excitement raced through Kendall. Kincaid wanted

her to visit Beth? Nothing would make her happier than an opportunity to speak to her best friend. The two of them frequently had long conversations to help each other make decisions, and she valued her friend's judgment. She'd love to know Beth's impression of Web.

"Do it in person," Web's boss suggested. "I want this contained."

At Kincaid's words, Kendall's excitement shattered, leaving shards of fear. Was *contained* a code word for *kill?*

"WHERE DOES BETH LIVE?" Web asked Kendall. While he'd finished his conversation with his boss, arranging for a package of supplies that included a vehicle to be delivered within the hour, Kendall had time to think, but as usual she'd been unable to come to a conclusion because she lacked data. Still, after they'd finished shopping for clothes, toiletries and a brunette wig for her in the hair salon, she realized that Web's Shey Group commanded resources unavailable to the common citizen.

When a salesman drove a one-year-old white Lexus RX SUV into the parking lot and handed Web the keys, she was amazed. When she looked over the supplies in the back that included three cell phones, weapons, a hefty amount of cash, computer equipment and telecommunications electronics she didn't even know the use for, she was doubly impressed.

"The salesman could be an ex-veteran or one of Kincaid's former buddies from NSA. Or someone who owes the Shey Group a favor." Web held open the passenger door and she slipped onto the leather seat, appreciating the cool air-conditioning. At the surprise that must have shown on her face, Web grinned. "Kincaid believes his people work better when he coddles them. If a brand-new vehicle wasn't so conspicuous, he would have purchased that instead."

The Lexus had that new smell, and she glanced at the mileage, not the least surprised to see it had less than three thousand miles. It seemed incongruous to her that a man who would spend this kind of cash on keeping them safe would be the same kind of man to order Web to kill her best friend. Besides, Web seemed to have too much honor to kill Beth just to shut her up.

And yet…as much as Kendall wanted to discount that possibility, she couldn't. By taking Web to see Beth was she putting her friend in danger from the Shey Group, or the people who were after her?

"Beth lives in an apartment with two roommates who will recognize me," Kendall lied. "Maybe I should call her."

Web pulled out of the parking lot. "Kincaid thinks an in-person visit is best, and the man has uncanny instincts. We'll do this in person and case the place before we go in."

"But—"

"Kincaid developed the antimissile defense code for NSA. He's tied to the CIA, and his contacts extend from the White House to the Kremlin. I take his suggestions as an order."

"And you always obey orders?"

"Yes." She liked that Web didn't mind admitting how much he admired his boss. "Unless the situation changes. Then I'm free to decide on the spot.

But Kincaid always keeps sight of the big picture. He's saved my life several times, risking assets and other men to extract me from a no-win mission. He looks out for me and I get well paid to do as I'm asked.''

''How come you're telling me all this?'' She scratched her scalp under the wig that was hot and itchy, but knowing she was less likely to be recognized, she kept it on.

''Despite what you told Kincaid, you still have doubts. Do I seem like the kind of man who would hurt your friend?'' As Web turned away from the center of town, he glanced at her, his gray eyes amused yet sincere.

That he understood her inability to trust him came as no huge revelation. After all, he was intelligent and observant. What did amaze her was his willingness to talk openly about her concerns. So she gave him an honest answer. ''I'm not willing to risk Beth's life on my impression of you. And what about your speech about not contacting my friends because it could put them in danger?''

''Your friend Beth is putting you in danger by her media blitz.'' Web drove past the country club golf course, in the opposite direction of Beth's condo. ''Do you know how to shoot a gun?''

His sudden change in the subject of conversation seemed to come out of nowhere. ''Why?''

''Suppose when we visit Beth, I gave you a loaded weapon to hold. Would that reassure you?''

She glanced at his muscular frame and frowned. ''Haven't you been trained to disarm someone like me?''

He chuckled. "Yes. But I would keep my distance."

She stared at him, took in his sincere expression and then shrugged in disappointment. "Well, it doesn't matter because I don't know how to shoot. Mom always hated guns. She said civilized folks should solve their differences with words. And she'd never have forgiven herself if one of the neighborhood kids had found the gun and shot someone by accident."

"A gun is a tool and can be used for good or bad depending on the person using it. A hammer can kill, but you probably had one of those."

"What's your point?"

"I'll teach you to shoot a gun." Amusement and challenge filtered into his tone. "Then I'll let you keep it."

"This from the man who didn't trust me with a knife?"

"Look, we're in this together. You didn't try to slip a note back at the farm. You didn't try to run or call for help at the store. If you believe me, then I can trust you with a weapon. And since we don't know what we're facing, I'd feel better if you could defend yourself."

"I don't know." Her gut churned with excitement at the prospect but she didn't want him to know that. Although she'd spouted her mother's views, it seemed to her that a gun could be a great equalizer between the sexes. So what if it was noisy? So what if it could kill? Some men needed killing. And if that made her bloodthirsty—so be it.

Back in the forest when someone was shooting at them, she'd have liked nothing better than to shoot back. And she appreciated that Web was encouraging her to take care of herself. Franklin had carried a weapon in a holster, and he'd always projected the I'll-take-care-of-you demeanor that she'd found patronizing.

While she'd never thought of carrying a weapon before, there had been no need until now. And while she didn't know if she could actually pull the trigger and shoot anyone, she suspected that she could and would do so in self-defense or to save someone she loved from harm.

"You needn't pretend with me," Web told her as if he'd read her mind. He had an uncanny knack for doing so that irritated her, although she didn't know why.

"Pretend what?"

"Any woman who fought me as hard as you did, back when the chopper landed, will adore shooting a gun. In fact—" he aimed his charming grin at her "—after I get done with you, you're going to feel naked without one."

He drove her to the shooting range outside of town. Empty in the middle of the day, they had the place to themselves. Then Web gave her a thorough indoctrination, teaching her safety rules before he even allowed her to touch the weapon. She learned the names for all the parts, how to stand braced and how to use the sights. He made her load the clip and then slide it home into the gun, until she could do so with her eyes closed. After donning earmuffs and safety glasses, he finally let her shoot, and she was pleasantly amazed that the gun barely kicked in her hand.

But she was shocked at how easy it was to hit a

target the size of a man from only ten feet away. Shooting in real life was much easier than it looked on television or at the movies. Web told her that striking a moving target was much more difficult, but after shooting through five clips of ammo, she had no doubt that if she was forewarned, she could hit anyone before they could reach her. After shooting through ten clips, her hand was pleasantly sore, her arm muscles quivered as if from a workout. Thanks to Web's knowledgeable tutelage, she no longer feared that she could shoot herself or anyone else by accident.

They cleaned the guns with oil, and Web fitted her with an ankle holster. She made sure her weapon was loaded with a bullet in the chamber, but on safety. She need only bend, yank out the gun and flick her thumb over the switch to be ready to fire.

As they drove back to Canfield to find Beth, Kendall prayed killing wouldn't be necessary. She especially didn't want to have to test her new skill. She especially didn't want to have to shoot Franklin.

Chapter Six

Web didn't like taking Kendall into town where, despite the wig, she could easily be recognized, and where Franklin had built up a network of contacts—but Kincaid had believed this stop necessary. Apparently Beth would continue to stir up trouble unless Kendall convinced her friend that she was okay.

On the way to Canfield, he counted five posters on telephone poles showing Kendall's face and promising a reward for tips that led authorities to her. And back at the shopping center, he'd seen her picture on the front page of the local paper with the headline Canfield's Runaway Bride.

Web hoped Kincaid would soon get a bead on what Franklin was thinking and doing. Yet, infiltrating the FBI when one suspected an agent of duplicity had to be tricky. However, if anyone could get results, his boss would be the one to accomplish it.

"Where does Beth live?" Web asked again, suspecting Kendall had lied to him the first time he'd asked that question. She wasn't a good liar and he felt certain it was from lack of practice. When she'd told him Beth had two roommates, Kendall had looked upward and to the left, her voice had tight-ened and the pulse in her graceful neck had esca-lated.

''She's in the penthouse condo over on the corner of Main and Pickle Street.'' Kendall pointed west. ''Turn left at the Y junction.''

''She doesn't have roommates, does she?''

An attractive pink tinged her cheeks. ''No. Sorry, I shouldn't have lied. It's been difficult for me to figure out what's really going on. I wanted to protect Beth.''

''I understand.'' And he approved of her instinc-tive loyalty. Web understood that kind of commit-ment. He'd risked his life many times for others in the Shey Group, and they'd done the same for him, forging bonds that he expected to last a lifetime. ''What about an alarm system?''

''I know the code.''

Knowing the alarm was there would prevent him from setting it off by accident. More important, he sensed that Kendall was trusting him more all the time.

He didn't elaborate that Kincaid had recently hired an expert jewel thief who considered breaking in to the world's finest museums a lark. After the man had finished training the entire Shey Group, not many locks would keep them out. ''But I'm hoping that when we knock on the door, she'll be home and invite us in. Tell me about Beth's place. Does her penthouse encompass the entire top floor of the building?''

''Yes. She's on the eighth floor.''

''Any other tall buildings around it?''

"Just the television station across the street where Beth works during the week. Why?"

"Just curious." He didn't want to mention that if he was in Franklin's position he'd have surveillance watching Kendall's best friend on the off chance Kendall might show up. "Does the building have a doorman?"

She chuckled. "This is Alabama."

"Yeah, right. Okay, you said no roommates. What about a boyfriend?"

Kendall shook her head and used the opportunity to scratch under the wig. "Not at the moment."

"Does her family have keys to her place?"

"Yes."

"Do they visit often? Pop in unannounced?"

"Yes and yes."

He refrained from groaning. Normally, he'd case the place, keep watch until he was sure Beth was alone, and he'd have help. But the Shey Group was spread thin right now, and he wouldn't ask Jack to return and miss being with his newborn and his wife when Web could manage on his own.

However, between the publicity and the towns-folk, he hated to risk anyone spotting Kendall. They'd have to wait for dark and go in fast. "Tell me about Beth's family and what they do for a living."

"Her brother's a karate instructor. Her mom's a cop, and her father's the head of the Harley Rough Riders."

For a moment, she had him going and then he burst into laughter. "Very funny. You want to try again?"

She smiled with him. "Her dad's the president of

the local bank. Her mom spends her time going from her manicurist to her physical trainer to the golf course. And her brother is away at college. Sound safe enough?''

''Any dangerous dogs on the premises?''

''Beth has a saltwater fishtank full of assorted neon fish and a cat named Whiskers. She's been declawed so you should be safe.''

He didn't mind Kendall making fun of his precautions. In fact, he preferred her levity to when she thought he might be going there to kill her friend. But for now, at least, she seemed to have made up her mind that he meant no harm—and for that he was grateful.

''Does Beth keep regular hours?''

''Usually yes, but if she's drumming up publicity trying to find me...I don't know.''

''Does she have any weapons on the premises?''

That earned him a cool glance of amusement from Kendall. ''Why?''

''I don't want her to shoot us. Me because she's scared. You because she doesn't recognize you.''

''Oh, she'll recognize me.''

''How can you be so sure?''

Kendall chuckled. ''Together Beth and I have tried bleaching and frosting and dying our hair every color under the sun.''

Okay. He would take her word for that and file it away. Beth's recognizing her friend could come in handy or blow their cover. Web had to be prepared for either eventuality. ''How many elevators are in the building?''

''Two.''

''Fire escapes?''

"One. On the south side of the building." She gazed at him, curiosity in her eyes. "Are you always this thorough?"

He snorted. "Thorough? This is the most superficial insertion I've ever done—especially when I'm supposed to be protecting you."

"Sorry I'm so much trouble," she said, not looking sorry at all. With her chin tilted at a cocky angle and her eyes gleaming with pleasure, he suspected she was looking forward to this visit with her friend.

He resigned himself to sharing her. Just because he liked being alone with her didn't mean she shouldn't visit with Beth. Web had never been the jealous type. In fact, he preferred women who had their own set of friends and interests.

He reminded himself that she wasn't his.

They had never gone on a date.

They hadn't kissed.

They barely knew each other, and he had no right to think of her in any way except as a client or as someone in need of protection. He reminded himself that just a few hours ago, she'd actually suspected he might harm her friend. But her suspicion didn't stop him from admiring her courage or her intelligence or her sexy curves. He especially enjoyed the way her eyes gleamed with excitement, revealing her capacity to care deeply about others.

He also didn't lie to himself. Their time together so far reminded him of combat—short and intense. They'd connected on levels he couldn't quite put into words. And if she was no longer fighting him, if she finally believed him, in part it was due to that connection.

He hoped he had no reason to break her trust. But

that would depend on Kendall's ability to placate her friend. He could get them in. The rest would be up to Kendall. Curious what she would say to her friend, he asked, "You going to tell Beth the truth?"

"I'M NOT SURE what to tell her," Kendall admitted, pulling her baseball cap down low over her eyes as Web turned onto Main Street and went around the block to survey the elegant, brick-and-glass condominium that screamed nouveau riche. She understood Web enough to know he was focusing more on the entrances and exits, the approaches where they would have cover and the areas they would be exposed, than their conversation.

What should she tell Beth? The truth seemed so unbelievable that it had taken her over twenty-four hours to come to grips with it. Web had not just convinced her with his words, but his actions and the manner with which he wielded power. He'd won Kendall over with logic and intelligence and tenderness, and she now believed Web to be exactly who he'd claimed—how could she not after he'd taught her to use a gun and was willing to let her hold it on him? But then she'd believed Franklin and he might have lied to her repeatedly. If she was truthful with herself, Franklin had swept her up in a whirlwind romance when she'd been at her weakest after her mother's death.

Now that she could compare Web's consistent behavior with Franklin's erratic nature, she'd come to realize that she may have been more enthralled with the idea of being in love than she was actually in love with Franklin. Had she wanted a family so much that she'd been willing to forgive Franklin's sudden disappearances that he'd claimed had been job-related without question? Had she also been willing to excuse his idea to put off lovemaking until after their wedding because she'd really believed the idea romantic? Now she thought it more than odd. Suspicious.

But should she tell Beth everything?

As if reading her mind, Web suggested, "Sometimes it's easier to believe a partial truth."

Kendall turned in the seat and studied his handsome face, his steady eyes, his straight nose, his firm lips that hesitated as if he knew how much she didn't want to lie to Beth. In the short time they'd been together, she suspected he already knew and understood her far better than Franklin had. Web was observant and he had an uncanny understanding of how her mind worked. "I don't want to put Beth in danger by telling her more than I must."

"Then you shouldn't say a word about your father. Or that we suspect Franklin is a double agent."

"I understand." She accepted his advice, fully believing he knew how to cover their tracks.

An hour after dark, they entered Beth's building and took the elevator to the top floor. While Kendall still hadn't settled on a story, an idea was niggling at her. Beth was a romantic at heart but she hadn't been in favor of this wedding. Although she'd never come right out and said anything against Franklin, she hadn't been wild with joy about the guy. So if Kendall could come up with a good enough reason for her change of heart, Beth would believe she'd had doubts about the marriage.

Kendall knocked on Beth's front door, her heart tripping. When Beth didn't answer, she pressed the touch keypad and the lock clicked open. Once inside, she tried to disable the alarm, but the blinking red light warned they had mere seconds until the alarm company would summon the police. "She must have changed the code."

"It's okay." Web smoothly took over. He opened the plastic box that housed circuits and wires, then attached an electric device that turned the alarm light to green, then snapped the box shut.

She was about to hit the light switch when he grabbed her hand. "Don't do anything that reveals we're here. And whatever story you tell your friend, remember to incorporate some reason for secrecy."

"Okay. Now what?" Edgy, standing in the dark, she shifted from foot to foot, her sneakers squeaking on Beth's marble floors. When Whiskers rubbed against her legs, demanding attention she picked up the cat. "Hi, fella. Miss me?"

Web plucked a tiny penlight from his front pocket. "We check the layout."

"The living room leads to a hallway and the master suite. The kitchen and spare bedroom are this way," she gestured, letting him pick the direction as she continued to hold and pet the cat. She found his soft purring soothing on her jangled nerves.

The exquisite rooms were large, the ceilings with crown molding high, and while Beth could have afforded a decorator, she'd chosen everything from the bamboo flooring to the Venetian-cut chandelier. The eclectic mix of priceless antiques and contemporary furniture, some rescued from a dumpster and lovingly refinished, portrayed Beth's quirky personality as much as two elaborate floral arrangements that revealed her artistry with lilies. As Kendall followed

Web down the dark hallway, she noted he wasn't just concerned with the layout. He checked every closet and under every bed, any place spacious enough for a man to hide. He examined the window locks and closed every blind, then tested the doors to the balconies as well as the pantry and the extra bathrooms, sliding back the shower doors to make sure the place was empty.

The lock at the front door clicked again, and Kendall jumped as if she was a cat burglar about to be caught. Whiskers leaped out of her arms and padded down the hall. Web put a warm, reassuring hand on her shoulder and suddenly she knew exactly what to tell her friend. When Beth stepped into her condo, alone, Kendall let out a huge sigh of relief.

"Beth? It's Kendall," she called out, afraid she'd give her unsuspecting friend a heart attack if she didn't identify herself.

Beth flicked on the light, her enormous brown eyes going wide, then her face breaking into a warm smile. Flinging herself into Kendall's arms, she half laughed, half sobbed, "Oh, God. I can't believe it's you." She hugged Kendall so tightly her ribs almost cracked. "How could you go off and not tell me anything? I thought you were dead. And Franklin's been out of his mind with worrying..."

"I know. That's why I came as soon as I could." Kendall soothed her while Web looked on, clearly curious how she would handle the situation and ready to play along.

"Beth, I want you to meet Web Garfield. Web, this is my best friend, Beth Patterson."

Web held out his hand, his expression friendly. "Pleased to meet you, ma'am."

Beth's brown eyes narrowed, but she shook his hand. "Thanks for bringing Kendall back safe to me."

"We can't stay long," Web said as Beth paused for breath, his look warning Kendall that the longer they stayed, the more danger they would put Beth in.

Kendall squeezed Beth's hand. "I came to reassure you that I was okay."

Beth closed the door, reset the lock and stooped to scratch Whiskers behind the ears. "So where the hell have you been? And what's with the atrocious wig? And how did you get past my alarm after I changed the combination?"

"Web has a way with electronics," Kendall answered vaguely and tugged off the wig. Beth may have been shaken up over her disappearance, but she was recovering quickly and she had a ton of questions in her sharp eyes.

Beth bit her bottom lip. "If I'm reading things right, electronics is not all Web has a way with."

"That reminds me." Web detached the alarm's plastic casing and then the device he'd inserted earlier. "I can remove this now." Noting Beth's confused look, Web added, "I didn't hurt anything. Your system's as good as new."

"It's not my system I'm worried about but Kendall." Beth gave Kendall one of her I-need-convincing looks, then entered the kitchen, poured Whiskers a bowl of food, replenished his water and washed her hands at the sink. Kendall knew her friend was stalling, her mind thinking a mile a minute, a trick she used often during her interviews to put people off guard. Beth pulled glasses from a cabinet, a wine bottle from the fridge, extracted chocolate Kisses from a cabinet, dumped potato chips into a bowl and brought everything to the coffee table. "Talk. And start at the beginning."

Kendall helped herself to a chocolate Kiss and a handful of chips. "Web and I met while I was away that semester at the University of Alabama."

"You never told me..." Beth hesitated to say more as if fearing Web might take offense. Kendall loved her friend for many reasons, but she appreciated her tact right now more than ever.

"Web wanted to get married, but I was set on finishing school." Kendall knew Beth would buy a romantic story, and Web played along without once changing expression, merely keeping his arm protectively over her shoulders for emphasis. "We fought and broke up. Then Mom—"

"Slow down. You're going way too fast." Beth sipped her wine. "You fought about getting married, and that's why you broke up?"

Web chuckled. "She was convinced there was nothing between us but...lust. I knew better."

Kendall almost spilled her wine over the heat he put into those words. And when she risked a glance into his gaze, her stomach did flip-flops until she reminded herself that he was acting to fool Beth. But, oh my, could the man turn on the charm.

"Then Mom died and I came back to Canfield," Kendall continued, wondering if she should have come up with a better story, especially since Web seemed so pleased with this one. "When Web heard I was marrying Franklin, he decided I was making a mistake."

"Well, that makes two of us," Beth admitted, eyeing Web with new appreciation.

"When I wouldn't take his calls, he decided on drastic measures and hijacked me on the way to my wedding."

"But you don't want me to call the police, do you?" Beth asked, hanging on Kendall's every word and frowning at Web. As much as Beth had disapproved of Franklin, she would take her cues from Kendall, making her realize how dear she really was.

Web pulled Kendall tight against him, presenting a united front. With her head tucked against his shoulder, her side nestled against his chest, she no longer needed her usual comfort foods. Especially when his scent was richer than chocolate and his touch heated her faster than sipping her favorite wine.

Web spoke in a reasonable tone. "What we want is for you to stop the media blitz. As you can see, Kendall is fine."

"Are you?" Beth stared at Kendall, her mind clicking into reporter mode, probing the story, seeking inconsistencies and weaknesses. "Are you really fine? And if so why haven't you called?"

"Because Web decided to leave by helicopter and we crashed in the—"

"Oh, my God!" Beth almost spilled her wine and set down her glass. "You were in that chopper? I showed the clips last night. There was just a black metal shell."

"We got out before it exploded," Kendall told her, feeling guilty for putting Beth through so much worry.

Beth reached for her cell phone. "Even if I don't like...you've got to call Franklin."

"I can't." Kendall shook her head, knowing this was the trickiest part of the story.

"Why not? You have the right to change your mind about the marriage, but not letting him know you are alive is downright irresponsible."

As Beth stared hard into Kendall's eyes, Web bailed her out. "Franklin isn't what he seems."

"I don't want him to find me. That's why I was wearing the wig. For a disguise."

"Excuse me?" Beth downed the rest of her wine in one gulp.

"Franklin went a little nuts," Web said, taking over the conversation for a moment. "Someone shot at us while we were in the forest. We think it might have been Franklin," Web lied for her. The shooter couldn't have been Franklin, and guilt stabbed her for blaming him when they knew from Kincaid that Franklin had been at the FBI office at the time. "With his FBI connections, Franklin has the resources to track us."

Beth frowned. "I don't understand."

Web scowled as if he found the notion distasteful. "There are men who believe that if they can't have a woman, no one else should."

"Are you saying Franklin has gone insane and is trying to kill Kendall?"

"We don't know." Kendall spoke softly. "Right now I don't want to talk to him. After all that's happened, I don't even want him to know I'm alive."

"Okay. Fine." Beth leaned forward and took Kendall's hand. "I'll do whatever you want. I'll put an end to the posters and television and radio and newspaper blitz, but you can't spend the rest of your life hiding.''

"She won't have to." Web spoke again. "I'll see to that."

"How?" Beth asked, her tone wary and challenging and sympathetic all at the same time.

Web's tone was self-assured. Solid. "You don't want to know."

Beth's eyes flashed. Clearly unsatisfied with Web's vague response, she was about to press him further when Web stood, his expression grim. He signaled for them to keep talking with a rolling motion of his hand, then mysteriously headed down the hall, merging with the shadows, his footsteps absolutely silent. But from the intensity on his face, the tightly pressed lips and the focused eyes, Kendall had no doubt he was stalking prey.

Someone must be in the apartment.

A shiver of fear shimmied down her spine. Had someone followed them? Were they in danger? If she'd brought trouble to Beth, she would never forgive herself.

And what about Web? Was he risking his life to protect them? While she had every confidence in his skills, he could be surprised or outnumbered.

Get a grip.

Kendall understood that Web had wanted them to keep talking while he checked out the disturbance, but she feared Beth was going to say something to give away Web's location. She put her finger to her lips, signaling Beth to be quiet. And then she pretended to talk to Web as if he was still in the room.

"Web, you're such a sweetheart for giving Beth and me this chance for girl talk." She prattled on and on, her head cocked, listening for some sign that Web was okay. When she couldn't think of another single syllable to utter, she stopped. And heard a crash, like glass smashing and bodies crashing into walls and furniture.

Web hadn't left her with instructions.

Should they hide?

Go help him?

Call 911?

Think.

She didn't have time to think.

No, she didn't have time to make a mistake.

From the crashing noises that echoed from the guest room and the sound of flesh smacking flesh, outside help wouldn't arrive in time. It was up to them to save themselves.

Idiot.

Kendall smacked her head with her palm still sore from her shooting lesson. How could she have forgotten the weight on her ankle or that she was armed?

Web had warned her not to pull her gun unless she was sure she could use it. Not to point it unless she wanted to hit her target. Not to pull the trigger unless she intended to kill. Web had also told her that hitting a moving target was much more difficult that a stationary one.

Oh, God. If she went down that hall, she had to make damn sure she didn't shoot Web by accident.

"Come on." Beth tugged her arm. "Let's get the hell out of here."

"Web might need help."

"Honey, if he can't defeat whoever broke in, you don't stand a chance."

"But I do." Kendall reached down to her ankle and withdrew the gun.

Chapter Seven

Web had aimed his weapon in front of him the moment he'd left the women behind him. From the living room, he'd already known someone had entered the apartment. If the rising fur on Whisker's back hadn't warned him, the sound of glass scraping would have. And as he approached, he took in a whiff of acid that would eat through glass and make breaking in a snap.

Had the shooter from the forest found them? Was it Franklin?

In the silence and darkness Web listened for the sound of breathing, the rustle of clothing, a board squeaking beneath the tread of a foot. Nothing. From the lack of sound he concluded the intruder was skilled, well trained, disciplined and deadly. Franklin had that kind of training. He wouldn't set off the alarms. He'd probably rappelled from the roof and had picked a bedroom at the far end of the penthouse to avoid being heard—which meant his surveillance was top-notch because he'd known in advance that his targets had been in the living area.

Hopefully the intruder would have no idea that Web's keen hearing had picked up that slight scraping of glass during the other man's initial entry. But Web was too experienced to count on surprise for an edge. One mistake, one wrong move could blow the mission. Even worse he was the only one preventing the intruder from getting to Kendall and Beth.

Kendall, bless her, had kept up a chatter, saying his name occasionally as if he were still in the room with them. He couldn't ask for her to do more and wondered how he'd been lucky enough to gain her full cooperation. In more ways than one, he was very glad he'd interrupted her wedding.

After reading Franklin's file, Web knew the man had had Special Forces training in addition to his FBI training. He'd be deadly with a gun. And if he was also a double agent, he may have received specialized hand-to-hand in any number of martial arts. Not for the first time on this mission, Web wished he had backup, someone to escort the women out the door while he stalked the intruder.

No worries.

Web cleared his mind of all distractions. Finally his eyes readjusted to the darkness. He could make out the blackness of the walls, the grayness of picture frames. Searching the deepest shadows for a glint of a weapon or the white of an eye or even the silhouette of a body part, he came up with zip. But that didn't mean the intruder wasn't here.

He sniffed again, hoping for a scent of soap, shampoo, cologne, aftershave. Nothing. Yet he sensed the man's presence like an ominous evil spinning a web of danger and waiting to draw him into its net.

In combat, time always slowed for Web. Elements

that passed by in minutes of real time seemed to take much longer under duress. Usually this allowed his mind to analyze every element and make the right decision. But with Kendall in the living room, the ticking seconds weighed heavily on his shoulders. How long before the women said or did something wrong? He feared most that they might come to investigate and wished he'd had the chance to give them instructions before he'd left them alone.

Too late now.

Instinct told Web the man was in the far bedroom, but in case he was wrong, he couldn't pass by the first bedroom without assessing and clearing it of danger. At all times he had to maintain his position between the intruder and his target.

While letting his gaze go back and forth between the hallway he'd vacated and the bedroom, he silently opened the closet, his gaze sweeping the empty balcony, then he ducked to see under the bed. Carefully he searched the bathroom. All empty.

Web crouched low and shifted into the hall. Something hard slammed down on his arm. Instead of pain, his fingers went numb and he dropped the weapon. He didn't waste his breath on a curse. Instead he rolled, lashed out with a foot and caught his foe in the ribs with a glancing blow. The guy had anticipated his move and avoided the direct force which would otherwise have broken the rib and punctured a lung.

Web's rolling maneuver should have ended with him balanced on the balls of his feet and facing his attacker, ready to go. But his opponent fired a weapon, the silencer muffling the shots, but nothing could disguise the bullets chewing up wood and plaster as they imbedded into the walls, floor and ceiling.

Down on his side, Web swiveled, scissors kicked and toppled the man. He heard a heavy object skid across the floor and hoped it was the gun. Out of the darkness, strong hands grabbed his throat, squeezed his jugular. Web slammed his good arm up in a strike to the other's forearms, but once again his opponent anticipated and blocked with a shift of his torso. And all the while those hands squeezed until Web's lungs burned for oxygen. Light-headed, with only one good arm, he had mere seconds to form a strategy.

Web went for broke. Bringing up his elbow, he rammed the man's nose, hard enough to break it but unfortunately not hard enough to ram the bones into the skull for a killing blow. As Web expected, the hands on his throat didn't loosen. With a roar of pain, the guy tightened his hold, but he dropped his chin to avoid swallowing blood.

That was the move Web had been waiting for. After reaching around the man's head and positioning his arm over the man's shoulder and chin, Web grabbed on to his own shirt for leverage. Then he began to squeeze in a choke hold.

Sensing his tactical mistake too late, his opponent attempted to slam Web's head into the marble floor. Web heard a resounding snap. And blacked out.

"KENDALL, THIS ISN'T a good idea." Beth tugged on the back of Kendall's shirt.

"I haven't heard a sound in over a minute." Her mouth desert dry, Kendall took another step forward, aiming the gun as Web had taught her earlier, her heart pounding so hard, her hands shook. "Web," she called out softly.

No one answered.

Kendall flicked on the hall lights. And at the sight of the two still bodies, Web's and a complete stranger's, her skin went clammy. "Oh, my God." She started to run toward Web, but Beth clamped a hand around her upper arm, tugged hard and halted her in her tracks. "Let me go. I've got to see if Web's...all right."

"No." Beth's eyes were wide with fear, her voice insistent. "Haven't you seen those movies where the villain pretends to be hurt and then rises up to attack the girl?"

"This is real life, not television."

"Television drama is based on real life. No way am I letting you—"

Kendall twisted her arm out of her friend's grasp and hurried toward the men who lay sprawled on the floor, their limbs twisted in disarray. Despite her fear and rising panic, Kendall couldn't run away when Web could be injured and might need help. "Beth, that other man's neck is broken. He's dead."

"You sure?" Beth, bless her, hadn't left her alone. She'd stayed, but at the other end of the hall, as if ready to flee at any moment.

As a precautionary measure, Kendall spared the man a second glance. No way could he still threaten them. He was big, bigger than Web, and as she took in his harsh features frozen in a death mask, she couldn't stop a shiver of revulsion. With his eyes open and glassy, his neck angled unnaturally, he was a goner. "He's dead. Dead. Barring divine intervention, he's not going to rise up and hurt anyone ever again.''

Dropping to her knees beside Web, she placed her ear over his heart. And heard nothing. Please, please, let him be alive, she prayed.

''Is he…?'' As if saying the words aloud could cause bad news, Beth clearly couldn't bring herself to finish her question.

''I don't know.'' First aid was not Kendall's forte. Her own blood was rushing so hard though her veins she couldn't hear Web's heartbeat.

Beth lightly put her hand over his lips. ''Well, he's still breathing. Now can we call 911?''

Yes. Oh, how she'd love to turn Web's care over to someone who knew what they were doing. She recalled how he'd helped her escape the crashed helicopter and fed her in the forest and wished she could do more for him now. But she knew he wouldn't want her to bring in outsiders. ''No.''

''What do you mean 'no'?'' Beth stared at her, her eyes blazing with irritation, fear and suspicion. ''Is there something you haven't told me?''

Kendall couldn't tell Beth about the Shey Group or Franklin's duplicity without putting her in more danger. She couldn't call for help because Franklin might have sent this man and would surely have the emergency channels monitored. And if he learned this killer had failed, he'd likely send another to finish the job. With Web hurt, he couldn't protect himself, never mind her.

Sensing what she did next would be critical to their survival, she gulped air into her lungs and blew it out slowly. They needed help, all right, but she had to do the right thing.

"Beth, get me your cell phone."

"Who you going to call?" Beth hurried down the hallway, talking over her shoulder.

"Web's boss."

Returning, Beth handed her the phone with a frown. "What does he do?"

"Not now." Kendall dialed the ten-digit number she'd memorized when she'd been in the phone booth with Web. Now she could use that information to help Web. "Hello, is this Logan Kincaid?"

"Yes. Please identify yourself and explain how you got this number."

"It's Kendall. Web is hurt. I didn't know what to do and I called you first."

"Are *you* all right?"

She dismissed Kincaid's concern, but his steady voice calmed her. "I'm fine, but I don't know what to do."

"Kendall, you did the right thing by calling me. I know you're scared, but tell me your situation. How badly is Web hurt?"

"I don't know."

"Is he unconscious?"

"I'm not a doctor, but he's not talking. For all I know he's in a coma. You've got to do something. We're at Beth's apartment, and someone broke in. There was a fight."

"Are you in immediate danger?"

"I don't think so. Beth and I are okay, and Web killed the other guy."

"Other guy? He's not Franklin?"

"No."

"Hold on, Kendall. I'm going to patch you

through to a friend of mine. Megan Slade is a medical doctor and part of our group.''

''Hurry. I don't like his color.''

''Hello?'' The doctor's voice came through the line. Her greeting was slightly fuzzy, her pleasant tone husky as if she'd just awakened in the middle of the night. But the three-way call was as clear as if the conversation was taking place in the same room.

''Web's unconscious,'' Kincaid explained tersely.

''For how long?'' the doctor asked.

''Maybe a minute or two,'' Kendall replied. ''I'm not sure.''

''Kendall's the woman Web's been protecting,'' Logan explained again.

''Hi, Kendall. Is Web's heart beating?'' Megan asked, her voice suddenly alert and practical.

Kendall leaned down and tried again in frustration while Beth looked on. ''I can't hear it.''

''Can you see his chest rising and falling?''

''Yes.''

''Don't move Web, but from his current position can you see any bleeding?''

''No blood. There's dark bruises on his neck.''

''All right, you're doing fine. Look at his neck. Can you see a spot where his pulse is throbbing?''

''No.''

''Touch his neck lightly below the ear with your pointer and index finger.''

''Okay.''

''Do you feel a throbbing?''

''Yes.''

''Excellent. I want you to start counting the throbs when I say go,'' Megan instructed. ''Ready?''

"Yes."

"Go."

One. Two. Three… She followed the directions, and Beth didn't say a word as if understanding that talking would throw off Kendall's concentration. Looking pale and shaky, her friend went into the bathroom and Kendall hoped she was okay.

"Stop."

"Fifteen beats."

"That's great. Web's normal pulse is sixty per minute and we timed him for fifteen seconds."

Beth came back from the bathroom, skirted around the dead body with a look of distaste and wariness and joined Kendall. "Beth is putting a damp rag over Web's forehead. Okay?"

"That's fine. Just don't move him."

Despite her worry, Kendall snorted. "That's not likely, Doc. If you'd ever seen the man, you'd know moving him would take a crane."

"I heard that." Web's eyes fluttered open.

"Kincaid, he spoke!" Kendall yelled with joy.

"Now if I could just get you to listen," Web jested and reached for the phone. He'd never seen that phone before, but he had no difficulty finding the speaker setting. "I just went out for a few seconds, boss. Pressure on the carotid artery will do that."

"You don't sound like yourself yet," Kincaid noted.

"Throat's a little sore."

"Do you have a headache?" the doc asked.

"No."

"Fuzzy vision?"

"No. In fact I'm gazing up at the most beautiful—"

"Any nausea?"

"No. I'm fine," he insisted.

"He sounds normal to me." Kincaid sounded relieved.

"Web, reach behind your head and gently touch your neck," the doctor directed. "Any sharp pain? Tenderness or swelling?"

"Nope. I don't think I hit my head, Doc. I was already on the floor when I blacked out."

"Understood. Okay, I'm clearing you to roll to your side."

Web rolled. "I'm good to go."

"Easy. I don't want you to risk falling and blacking out again by getting up too fast. Slowly sit up."

Web followed the doctor's directions and Kendall braced herself to catch his head if he suddenly slumped. "I'm sitting up. Oh, sh—"

"What's wrong?" Megan asked, the doctor's tone sharp. "Is his neck floppy? Is he vomiting? Did he pass out? Someone talk to me," she demanded.

"I'd answer if you'd let me get a word in edgewise," Web almost snarled. "I'm okay, Doc. My expletive was because I finally got a look at my assailant's face."

"You know him?" Kincaid astutely guessed.

"Yeah. He's an old army buddy, Nate Ryson. We went through…training together. When he washed out, he threatened to get even with me, but I always thought it an empty threat."

Kendall slumped against the wall, unable to keep her escalating anger from erupting. "Are you saying Franklin didn't send this guy after us?"

"I'll get the lowdown on any connections between Franklin and your Mr. Ryson and get back to you," Kincaid said. "Megan, are we done here?"

"Yes. Take two aspirin and call me in the morning, Web."

"Thanks, Doc."

"What about Nate's body?" Beth asked.

"I'll send someone over to clean up," Kincaid promised, "and pay for all the damages to your premises, of course."

Beth looked from Web to Kendall. "We need to call the cops. I don't want to be accused of being an accessory to murder."

Web tried to reassure her. "The Shey Group will take care of everything—"

"That's not good enough."

"Beth." Kendall's sharp tone caught her friend's attention. "Let them handle this their way."

Beth frowned. "You sure?"

"Yes."

Feeling as if her life were unraveling, Kendall made her tone confident. She didn't want Beth to have to deal with their mess. But she didn't know what to think. Just when Web had finally convinced her that Franklin was a traitor and a murderer, she learned they might have been totally off base.

But it was also possible that Kendall had been in danger only because she'd been with Web. If Nate had come after Web on some personal vendetta, she'd simply been in the wrong place, with the wrong person at the wrong time. Nate hadn't cared about shooting her—only Web.

One thing she knew for sure. Whether Franklin was connected to Nate in some way—the wedding was off. She couldn't have ever truly loved Franklin if Web could put this many doubts in her mind. True love required one to believe in the other person—no matter what.

If Web had told Kendall that Beth, rather than Franklin, had been a traitor, no way would she have believed him. About Beth, Web could have shown her documents, and she'd have believed them to be forged. He could have shown her a film, and she would have figured it was Hollywood magic. She believed in Beth one hundred percent—but that was not the situation with Franklin. So marrying him would have been a huge mistake.

However, she wasn't as sure what to think about Web and the Shey Group. Kendall stared at Web, wondering what the hell was going on, because her ex-fiancé sure hadn't been the one chasing or attempting to kill them as she'd assumed.

Web shoved to his feet. He didn't wince, but lumbered to stand in a manner that struck her as more painful than he was admitting. Whether that pain was due to injuries or to finding out that he might have kidnapped her for no good reason, she couldn't tell.

Despite his discomfort, his tone remained even, his thoughts logical. "Ryker Stevens is Kincaid's computer whiz. He'll run a diagnosis that will trace the lifetime whereabouts of Franklin and Nate, searching places they might have met. From preschool to college frat houses to training in the service—if they served together, Ryker's program will find a connection."

"And if he doesn't find a connection?" Beth asked.

Web leaned against the wall but his color remained good, his stance steady. "Lack of a connection either means there isn't one...or they covered their tracks with extraordinary care."

The ring of the doorbell interrupted their conversation. Web headed down the hall, his pace deliberate but even. "I'll get it. It's probably the cleanup crew. Don't touch anything."

As if they'd touch the dead body. When she so much as glanced at it, Kendall's stomach churned. And she saw questions in Beth's eyes and appreciated that she didn't ask them. "Beth, I'm so sorry to have brought this kind of trouble with me."

"It's not your fault." Her face pale, Beth glanced from the dead man to the Shey Group's team of forensic specialists entering her home. "All the same, I think I'll spend the night with my folks. Stay the night here if you want. Lock up when you leave."

"You sure?" Kendall didn't want to kick her friend out of her home. But the farther Beth was away from them, the safer she would be. Since she'd been with Web, the chopper had crashed, someone had shot at them and now an assassin had come after Web. The farther her friend was away from her, the safer she would be.

"Very sure." Beth gave her a hard, quick hug. "I won't say anything to Franklin or anyone else—until you give me the word."

"Thanks, Beth." Kendall embraced Beth in return, her eyes brimming with unshed tears, her throat clogged around a lump of emotion. Beth had stood by her, done as she asked and had held up like the true friend she'd needed.

Before Beth departed, Kendall gave her friend their new cell phone number, but still, a loneliness crept over Kendall and chilled her despite the warm air flowing into the penthouse through the window Nate had broken. The men who had arrived to remove the body asked her surprisingly few questions, but she assumed Web had filled them in and that Kincaid had pulled strings because the crime scene and forensics investigators finished and departed with the body in short order, leaving Kendall alone with Web.

He'd poured her a glass of wine but he drank bottled water. "Go ahead. You deserve to take the edge off."

"What about you?" She sipped, appreciating first the fragrant bouquet, then the rich heat that warmed a trail down her throat.

"Alcohol and head injuries don't mix."

She frowned at him. "You told the doc that your head was fine."

He nodded, his lips pulling upward into a grin. "Nothing a good night's sleep and a few aspirin won't cure."

He hadn't been completely truthful with the doctor, and Kendall suspected there was much more to the story between him and Nate that he also hadn't revealed. "Web?"

"Yeah."

"Do you think Franklin hired Nate to kill you?"

"No."

Web's blunt answer shocked her, especially because it didn't serve his purpose to sway her to his side. Certain he'd responded honestly, she sipped her wine and eyed him over the brim. His bronzed color had returned, his eyes appeared focused, yet reserved, and she wondered exactly what was going through his mind. "Why don't you think there's a connection between the two men?"

"It's unlikely Franklin just happened to hire a man who hated me."

"I suppose that makes sense." She was amazed at how Web analyzed the motivation from other people's points of view. But then, he'd always seemed to read her quite well, too, so she shouldn't have been all that surprised.

"Nate had the training to sabotage the chopper," Web elaborated. "He also hated me with a fervor few people would understand. But I doubt Franklin hired Nate to do his dirty work. However, Ryker's programs have proved me wrong before. Still, even with Franklin's FBI resources, it's unlikely he was on to our interest in him until *after* we interrupted your wedding."

"No matter what happens, I want to thank you for that."

Web's eyes widened. "I don't understand."

She sensed he'd been honest with her and, wanting to reciprocate, looked him straight in the eyes. "We weren't right for each other."

"You were going to marry him." Web's tone was gentle, curious and husky. And his gaze was warm and compassionate, yet flickered with questions he didn't ask.

"After my mother's death, I was grieving. Coming so close to dying, when that chopper went down, shocked me to my senses. If I'd loved Franklin enough, I wouldn't have believed he could betray his country. But I think he's guilty…" She swallowed back the last of her disappointment. "Why did Nate hate you enough to try and kill you?"

"Much of the story's details are classified." Web hesitated, then offered, "But I can fill you in, if you don't care about the particulars."

Knowing his story would help distract her from her sadness over the wedding that would never be, she nodded. She'd appreciate almost any story that would divert her thoughts from how close she'd come to making a bad mistake with Franklin. "Tell me what you can."

Web closed his eyes for a moment as if recalling the moment, then opened them and began to speak in a well-modulated tone that always made whatever he said interesting. "We were overseas, competing and training for a mission."

"Competing?"

"Only the best would be chosen. Life was Spartan, downright severe. If there were two ways to accomplish a training task, an easy way and a hard way, we always took the hard way. We didn't take shortcuts. We always gave total effort. We expected the most of ourselves and the men who were with us. Our lives depended on one another and mostly we trusted one another."

"I suppose since I haven't lived in those conditions I can't really understand." She had no difficulty imagining Web and his steady strength being an asset to whatever group he joined. Men would sense his honesty and be drawn to it as she was.

"Life was so difficult that most men failed to complete the first week, and the instructors kept weeding out those who didn't stay on task. We trained on one-quarter rations with less than thirty minutes of sleep a day and fifty-mile marches over harsh terrain, each man carrying an LBE.''

''LBE?''

''Load-bearing equipment. It consists of a pistol belt in a shoulder harness to which is attached an assortment of gear. A magazine, first-aid pouches, strobe light, compass, knife or bayonet, plus other assorted paraphernalia.''

''It's heavy?''

He nodded. ''Especially in the heat or rain and trudging through the muck. After a mind-numbing month of training, one day was particularly exhausting. We'd been moving hard through the night while it was cool, before the sun came up to suck the moisture from our bodies. We anticipated that with sunup, we'd take a rest, eat a few bites, get a chance to change our socks. We were all hungry, low on sleep, moving on our last reserves of energy. Tempers were frayed and tattered. I concentrated on simply putting one foot in front of the other, determined not to drop out—because we could quit at any time. All we had to do was say 'enough.' And in every way possible they encouraged us to quit. Once while our stomachs growled with hunger, they marched us past steaks grilling on the barbecues. Even now—at the memory, my mouth salivates.''

''It sounds like torture.'' She didn't understand that kind of dedication and willpower on anything but an intellectual level. Nevertheless, she could admire the kind of man it would take to voluntarily put himself through those kinds of grueling exercises. One thing was very clear to her, no matter how much he was telling her, she was just as sure he'd left out much more.

"It's necessary to weed out the men who aren't suited for that kind of work."

"Only the strong survive?"

"Yes."

"So what happened?"

"We finally reached the end of the march—and I doubt I could have taken another ten steps. When they said stop, I stopped and simply sat down where I was. Instead of the thirty minutes of rest that were nowhere near enough time to recover, five minutes later, we were instructed to pick up our new orders for the day. I barely found the strength to push back to my feet. My bones ached, my muscles didn't want to obey my mind. But somehow I stood and stumbled over to receive my new orders, praying I could find the strength to get through one more hour. And then I read the orders—that I had passed the final test. Me and the men around me broke into loud laughter. It was a celebration of relief, accomplishment and success."

"And Nate?"

"Nate quit—right before he picked up the order that he thought would send him on another march. Poor bastard. He made it through weeks of hunger and training and sleepless nights. He finished all the hard parts. And then he caved."

She imagined Nate would be ashamed and frustrated. "But why did he blame you?"

"He thought we were laughing at him. I was so damn tired, I hadn't even realized he'd quit until he attacked me." Web rubbed the bump on the bridge of his nose. "His first punch caught me off guard. He broke my nose, and he was what the Army would have called dishonorably discharged from our unit.

Only traitors attack a man in their unit. So, not only did he fail to make the special team, he was kicked out of our…group. But I never suspected he'd held a grudge all these years.''

Web's story helped her understand the kind of man he was. Although the man hadn't been after her, Web had believed he meant her harm and he hadn't hesitated to risk his life to protect her. From the deliberate tilt of his head and the dark bruises on his neck, she knew his neck must be sore as hell, but he hadn't spoken a word of complaint. After all he'd done today, the least she could do was to try to ease his pain. Very deliberately she set down her glass of wine, strode behind where he sat on the sofa and placed her hands on his shoulders.

He tilted his head back, locked gazes with her, his tone one of lazy challenge. ''What do you think you're doing?''

Chapter Eight

At Web's question, Kendall's eyes brightened and her cheeks flushed, but she didn't back down. "It's simple. You're hurting. I want to help. Don't read anything more into my offer, Web."

Her fingers closed over the tight muscles of his shoulders and worked on the knots of tension. She had a gift for finding each sore place and slowly digging into the muscle until the tautness relaxed into a much more pleasant ache. Despite what she'd said, there was nothing simple about her. However, if she wanted to hold on to her naiveté, he certainly had no intention of disabusing her of the notion.

Besides, her hands on his neck felt too good for him to do more than accept whatever she wanted to give him. However, knowing himself as he did, he realized that he already wanted more from her. He ached for her to lean forward and angle her mouth to his, longed to know how she would taste, wondered if her kiss would feel as good as her hands working the kinks out of his neck.

Web had had two serious relationships in his life. He liked women, enjoyed talking to them and had no problems with committing to one person. He imagined himself happily settled down one day with a bunch of kids. But that future was always far in the distance, like the milestone of passing his fortieth birthday. Sure it would happen, but not for almost a decade.

While Web had no difficulty with his work for the Shey Group and a relationship in his down time, the two women he'd been serious about couldn't cope with his absences. Rarely had he been able to call in or e-mail like men in the military. Nor could he discuss his work, and both women had found his secretiveness aggravating. One had cheated on him, the other had simply told him he had to choose between his career and her. Three years later he had no solutions and no prospects.

However, he'd seen other men cope with both marriage and work. Jack Donovan's wife, Piper, seemed to have little difficulty accepting Jack's absences. But then, she was a cop who obviously had similar values. Ryker Stevens's wife ran a multi-million-dollar floral business and kept quite busy during his missions, proving that marriage and a career with the Shey Group weren't mutually exclusive. Still, it was difficult enough to find the right woman *without* a career that could call him away at a moment's notice for months at a time.

Kendall's fingertips rubbed the sensitive spots around his ears and he let out a soft groan. "That feels good."

"You don't pamper yourself much, do you?"

"Pampering takes time."

"And money."

"Kincaid pays us quite well." In fact, Web had built more than a modest portfolio balanced by stocks, bonds and real estate so that whenever he retired, he could do as he pleased.

"Are all of your missions…dangerous?"

"Actually, most missions are long spurts of killing time under boring conditions between infrequent bursts of high-octane activity."

"But that's what you live for—the adrenaline high of risking your life?" She didn't sound as if she was condemning him, but she didn't sound enthusiastic, either.

"Perhaps," he admitted. Despite his interest in her, he wanted her to understand what made him tick and what he enjoyed. He didn't have time for games or misleading her. He really didn't want to begin another relationship unless the woman understood up front about his career. "There's a great satisfaction from using the skills I've learned—like a race car driver who takes the perfect curve. Or a gymnast who times a perfect landing."

"Or a general who plans a perfect battle?"

"Now you've got it," he teased. "And if more of my combat missions ended like this one, I'd be more eager to return home." He gazed up at her. "So now that your marriage is off, what are your plans?"

"My mother's illness interrupted my education. I'm going back to school to finish college." She sounded self-assured, as if she'd thought out her future and knew exactly what she wanted. "And meanwhile, I'll keep temping."

"Temping?"

"Taking temporary employment."

"What kinds of jobs have you done?" he asked.

"Secretarial work mostly. But I've temped as a

waitress and a cashier. I've picked pecans. I've delivered rental cars and newspapers. I've cleaned pools and boats, and once when my boss at the agency was away on vacation, I ran the agency and handed out assignments. Someday I plan to open my own temp agency.''

"What did Franklin think about your plan?"

"I never told him."

"You never told him?" Web tilted his head back to look at her, but she avoided his gaze.

She shrugged. "Franklin never asked. I suppose I never said anything, but instinctively I knew he wouldn't approve. He had some old-fashioned values that I figured I'd change after we married. Which just goes to show how poorly I was thinking. People don't change. I've read books that say one's personality is ninety percent set by age two."

"That still leaves the other ten percent."

She grinned down at him. "Nope, the rest of us are set by the time we're six. And I knew this. But Franklin told me what I wanted to hear. I suppose I returned the favor. After Mom's death, I didn't want any more conflict in my life. I just drifted and was content to let Franklin make all our plans for the future. I don't know what was the matter with me. What was I thinking?"

"You were grieving."

"That's no excuse for turning off my brain."

"Don't be so hard on yourself. Franklin fooled espionage experts for years. He's trained to manipulate people, and after your mother's death you were vulnerable."

"Beth tried to tell me..." Kendall gently pushed his head down and urged him to lean forward, a movement that gave her better access to his spine. Her fingers worked downward, easing sore spots he hadn't known he had. But now he couldn't see her face and had to interpret her mood from her tone as she asked, "Have you ever lost anyone close to you?"

"I lost my grandparents and mother before I was born. But I don't remember that."

"Do you have other family besides the brothers you told me about?"

"Aunts and uncles. A whole bunch of cousins. Plus nieces and nephews—so many I lose count."

"I can't imagine…"

He heard the wistfulness in her tone. He loved his brothers and enjoyed his cousins, but he was always eager to leave after his frequent visits. "Well, it's not all wonderful. Not a week goes by where someone isn't mad at someone."

"I once read that the opposite of love isn't hate—but indifference. Anger just proves that your family cares about one another."

"I suppose they do." He leaned back and tugged her around the couch until she sat next to him. He ached to take her into his arms and tell her that she wasn't alone, that he was here for her. But she wasn't ready to hear the words. "I know Beth assumed we would stay the night, but after a shower and a meal, we need to get out of here."

She didn't argue but accepted his leadership and he appreciated it. "Where are we going?"

"Someplace no one will find us." He grinned at her, a manly, charismatic grin that told her he enjoyed her company.

"And where would that be?"

"How would you like to spend some time at Polaris?"

She chuckled. "Perhaps that fall did more damage to your head than we thought. You want to hide out at the North Pole?"

ONE WEEK LATER, Kendall had explored Polaris, a high-end spa that catered to the South's rich and famous. When Web had suggested hiding out, she'd figured on some isolated mountain hideaway, not a top-notch spa in the northern part of the state, where she'd seen a country music star, a rodeo champion and several politicians in the spacious hallways. With no more stories about her on the news and this far north, she hoped no one would recognize her. While Web's bruises had faded, the Shey Group had treated her to a minivacation and she'd enjoyed everything from the natural hot springs to the world-class cuisine to horseback rides at sunset.

But her best memories would be the time she'd spent with Web. Although she wondered how long hiding out was going to take, pretending to be man and wife in the spacious suite of rooms had certainly proved no hardship. Web always acted the gentleman. He was attentive, but not clingy, and always protective. And the first few days had given her an opportunity to catch up on sleep.

But as luxurious as her surroundings were, Kendall was uncomfortable about her growing feelings toward her protector. In her eyes, he was just about perfect. But she'd shown her judgment hadn't been good with Franklin, and now she didn't know if she could trust herself.

She wished she was one of those women who

could just have a fling, without a million uncertainties getting in the way. But she valued people too much, valued herself too much, not to stop and think about consequences. She'd once believed Franklin's suggestion to wait to make love until after the wedding had been romantic. But, contradictorily, she also believed that the heat in Web's eyes every time he glanced at her was romantic.

She needed to talk to Beth, but Web had asked her not to phone anyone. She wouldn't go against his wishes—not with their lives at stake. With no end in sight to either catching Franklin or ending her time away from home, her impatience over her situation grew. And her sexual frustration was amplified by the beautiful lush setting of the spa, constant interaction with Web and too little work.

Usually she could take her mind off things by cleaning, cooking, working, window-shopping or talking to Beth. Here she had none of those distractions. And as nice as their suite was, it was beginning to feel like a prison.

Eager to talk to Web about how long they would need to stay at the resort, she entered the weight room. Although he worked out daily, she'd never approached him here, usually taking this time to walk or read the newspaper. She heard the clink of weights before she rounded the corner and saw him.

Oh, my.

At the sight of him stripped to the waist and wearing low-cut shorts, with his massive chest glistening as sunlight played off the bronze of his skin, her mouth went dry. Sweat poured down his face, emphasizing the hard line of his jaw, the angled cheekbones and the corded muscles of his chest.

When he saw her, he set down the weights, swiped a towel from the bench, wiped his face, then slung it around his neck. "Hi. Is something wrong?"

"N-no. Why?" She tried to appear as casual as he, but obviously she wasn't doing a very good job of concealing her interest. Her attempt to keep her eyes on his failed, and her gaze roved over that magnificent chest that was simply too much temptation.

He chuckled. "You have a pleased gleam in your expression. Like a thirsty cat who just fell into a bowl of cream."

"If you say so."

"Give me a minute and I'll be right with you." He removed the weights from the end of the bar and replaced them on a rack.

"Take your time."

She watched his every move, unable to look away. The light slanted over his muscles, creating a hunger in her that left her startled by its intensity. Their forced proximity had made her comfortable with him, but now with her tongue twisted in a knot, her nerves on edge, she felt as if she were sixteen again and left to the mercy of her hormones.

So what if he was a beautiful man? So what if she secretly lusted after him? She didn't have to act upon her feelings.

With Franklin, her decision to be with him had been based on the belief he was good for her and what she needed. Depending on her practical side obviously hadn't been such a good judgment call, but that didn't mean she should go overboard in the other direction and let her hormones make another bad choice.

However, the idea of Web being a bad choice

seemed ludicrous. Besides being gorgeous and protective, he was intelligent, kind, compassionate and had a good sense of humor. He even tolerated her sarcasm. So what would he think of her kisses?

As he joined her, looking so fine that her breath caught, she couldn't help angling her head upward, couldn't prevent the yearning in her eyes, couldn't stop her pulse from pounding in anticipation. She wouldn't make love to him, she promised herself. She just wanted one kiss to convince herself that reality couldn't match her fantasy.

Web didn't hesitate. In fact, he almost acted as if he'd been waiting for this moment, and recognizing her willingness, he slanted his mouth over hers. For a first kiss he was achingly smooth. His nose didn't smash hers, his lips settled at exactly the right angle.

She inhaled his pleasant male scent and his minty breath and then sighed. *Oh, my.* The man knew how to kiss. He teased, he taunted, he took. And pleasure swept her into a whirlwind of need. She couldn't seem to get enough of him.

But all too soon he pulled back. "Sorry. Let me shower and we'll pick up where we left off."

"Yes. No. I don't know." Damn. What had she done? The reality hadn't matched the fantasy. Oh, no. The reality had been *better.* Her skin felt electric, as if the current between them had generated some kind of irresistible electromagnetic bond she couldn't counter.

He swept her into his arms so fast that she let out a yelp. "What are you doing?"

"Do you think I'm crazy enough to leave you alone until you convince yourself you don't need another kiss?"

"Huh?" Another kiss? Was he crazy? She had yet to recover from the last one. But she couldn't think with her body at this angle and all the blood rushing to her head.

His eyes charmed, his smile coaxed, his tone demanded. "Shower with me." Without waiting for an answer, he carried her into the walk-in shower.

"Web, I have clothes on."

He chuckled. "That's one problem I know how to fix." He lowered her to her feet, letting her slide down his chest.

In automatic response, her pulse leaped as if primed, and she could have sworn her breasts swelled. Yet she wasn't ready for lovemaking, was she? She'd barely been prepared for that incredible kiss. She hadn't had time to comprehend just what he'd done to short-circuit her resistance to him, but whatever it was she had to figure it out before she gave in to madness.

Because kissing him again would be madness. Breathing in more of his scent would be insane.

So call her crazy. Reaching up, she placed one hand on either side of his head and guided his lips back to hers. Taking her action as all the permission he needed, he required no further encouragement. This time his kiss was just as devastating because he took more time. Nipping her top lip, nibbling the bottom one, he explored her mouth with a thoroughness that left her floored, dazed and tingling from the crown of her head to the soles of her feet.

She drank him in, pressing herself against him, reveling in the contained power of him. When her breath grew ragged and her lungs burned, she broke the kiss, swallowing back a thousand unspoken questions. She wanted to demand answers. But, more important, she wanted his mouth back on hers, his arms around her, his hips cradling her.

As if starved for affection, she couldn't get enough of his potent combination of heat and tenderness. She didn't know she could feel both wanton and cherished at the same time. She didn't know her blood could sing so loudly the melody overwhelmed whispered doubts. She didn't know that she could be so eager to take off her clothes.

No virgin, she'd made love with her high school flame. But she'd never known the kind of heady desire that had her hands threading into Web's thick hair to keep him close. Never had dispensing with clothes seemed so natural.

Web didn't fumble, but caressed and unbuttoned, unsnapped and unfastened in the same smooth manner he accomplished every task. Even the water from the shower rushed out at a soothing temperature. Refreshing, the water rained from two sides and four showerheads, sluicing over her flesh but failing to cool the heat his kiss had stoked.

But nothing aroused her as much as his smoky gray eyes and his clever hands, which he expertly directed over the arch of her back, the dip at her waist and the roundness of her bottom. She leaned into him, appreciating the slip and slide of his firm flesh against hers. When he soaped his hands and then covered her breasts, she'd never felt more lush or bawdy. Leaning back, needing to steady herself against the wall, she gave him free access.

"You have a beautiful body," he told her, bending down to skim his lips over her neck. And all the while, he lathered her breasts with soap, paying careful attention to her sensitive nipples. "Do you like this?"

A tingle ripped through her and she let out a soft groan. "Apparently, I do."

"You sound surprised."

"I haven't done anything like this in a very long time," she admitted. "Franklin wanted to wait until after we married."

"Hell, didn't you suspect something was wrong?"

"At the time I thought he was being romantic."

At her words he stopped caressing her breasts, took her hands in his. "I'm rushing you, aren't I?"

"Yes."

He groaned in frustration, like a kid about to lose his favorite treat. "I don't want to stop."

"Then don't stop." She threw caution away like an old pair of once-comfortable jeans that had grown too tight.

Confusion warred with desire in his eyes. "But—"

"Shh. Who said rushing is a bad thing?" Reaching for the soap, she worked up a lather and then finally she placed her hands on his chest. "You have no idea how much I've wanted to touch you."

"Is that so?" He chuckled and held still, letting her have her way with him.

"Oh, yes," she muttered, unable to restrain her eagerness. "You have the most magnificent chest and shoulders. That night when I rubbed you I couldn't help noticing."

"You noticed before that," he teased. "Didn't you think I saw you ogling me—"

She laughed and tweaked his nipples. "I do not ogle."

"If you say so." His tone turned low, husky, seductive, and she wondered why she had been fighting herself. What had she been thinking? Why had she been depriving herself when she could have been kissing and touching and...

She gulped.

Was she really going to make love to him?

She was. Because she couldn't think of one good reason not to.

Yet no matter how much she wanted him, she wouldn't risk getting pregnant. After spending her entire life abandoned by her father, she wouldn't gamble on accidentally bringing a child into the world without a solid union. "Web, I'm not on the pill."

She was surprised when he quickly slipped from the shower. Through the clear glass door, she saw him fumble for a box on the counter before he returned.

He held up a silver foil packet. "Kincaid sent them with the other gear. I found a box packed between the toothpaste and deodorant."

"What? How could he know that you and I..."

"He didn't. It's part of our equipment like our weapons or communication gear." She must have revealed what she thought of his boss sending in that kind of equipment because gentle amusement glimmered in Web's eyes. "Just because we have them doesn't mean we use them."

She would accept his statement at face value. It would be mean-spirited of her to condemn his boss when she was about to put his gear to good use. She took the packet from Web with a grin. "We are going to use them. All of them."

He made a mocking gasp and placed his hands over his heart. "I'm not sure I'm up for that, ma'am."

She glanced downward to his erection. "I'd say you are."

"I'll do my best."

She opened the packet and rolled the protection over him. His skin flexed at her touch. So warm. So hard. So slick. "Web?"

"Yeah."

"You'll need to go slowly. It's been a long time for me."

"No problem." He said the words easily, and she believed him. Whether in a crashing helicopter, while under fire, or while holding her in his arms, Web always kept control of himself.

He didn't disappoint her. "I don't want to rush you."

"Fine, then." She shot him a mischievous smile. "I'll take my time."

He let her touch him wherever and however she wanted for as long as she wanted. And she wanted to memorize the planes of his chest with her hands, wanted to revel in the differences between his hardness and her softness. She wanted to appreciate all the nuances of making love to him, his male scent that mixed with soap and water and seemed to envelop her in a haze of steam. His eyes turning to smoke as she explored his flat stomach and powerful hips. His mouth that quirked and tensed and swooped to recapture hers in another glorious kiss.

She snuggled against him, and with her breasts

warmed by the heat of his chest, her loins pressed against his erection, she suddenly had the most urgent need to take him inside her. Parting her legs, she reached for him to make it happen, but he scooped her into his arms. She felt like a kid in a candy store who'd just been deprived of a treat.

"Hey." She threw her arms around his neck. "Where are we going?"

"To do this properly."

At the intensity of his expression, she giggled. "There's a proper way to make love?"

"Damn straight."

She raised an eyebrow. "Really?"

"Oh, yes. We have two perfectly good king-size beds in this suite."

"But we're all wet."

As he carried her out of the shower and through the bathroom, he snagged a washcloth. "So I'll dry you."

She chuckled at the washcloth. "Um, that's not a very big towel."

"Exactly." He shot her a wolfish grin. "Drying you with a washcloth will take longer than with a towel."

"You…have a wicked…mind."

"You have no idea." She hadn't expected him to agree so happily.

But he was as good as his word. Better maybe. When they arrived in the bedroom, he lowered her to her feet, swept the coverlet and blanket off the bed while she closed the louvered wooden blinds. Not that anyone could see into their fourth-story room, she just felt a little less shy without the bright daylight outside revealing all the curves of her body.

"Come here," he commanded.

She didn't think of refusing. Not when every bare cell of her skin quivered for his touch. Putting aside her concerns about soaking the sheets, she flung herself at him, toppling him to the bed, no doubt upsetting his plan to dry her, but she couldn't seem to stop herself. She rarely had premonitions, but she had the strongest feeling that if they let too much time pass, they'd miss this opportunity.

"Please, Web. I want you now."

"Then you shall have me." Tossing aside the washcloth, he grinned up at her. "You can have anything you want. All you need do is ask."

She never understood what came over her. She had no explanation for her boldness—except that Web encouraged her to take all she wanted. She straddled his hips and then inch by inch she took him inside her, marveling how he filled her.

And then as he urged her on with his skillful fingers, she rocked her hips, enjoying the freedom of setting the pace, of taking what she wanted from a man so willing to give.

And when the sweetest orgasm burst over her, she collapsed on top of him. He held her close, his hand in her hair, his lips on her forehead, letting her ride out the spasms and come back to herself to discover he was still hard inside her.

His words dared her. "Ready for more?"

"What have you got?" she teased back, eager to see how far they could go together.

Surprised by the tenderness still in his eyes, she accepted that being with Web was much more than sex for her. Her feelings might be as muddy as a puddle after a summer storm, but being with Web felt good. Felt right.

She remained on top, but he took control, bucking his hips, sliding in and out of her, rekindling her heat. When his hands found her breasts, pleasure ripped straight to her core. And as they scaled the pinnacle of desire, this time together, she held on to him tightly, accepting that her growing feelings for Web might be the best thing that had ever happened to her.

Chapter Nine

After making love all afternoon, Web and Kendall were taking a nap. When the ringing of the cell phone roused him, Web came fully awake. Kendall appeared to be sleeping so soundly that he padded into the living room before answering, so as not to wake her.

With an unfamiliar number on the caller ID, he didn't bother to keep the gruffness from his tone, sure that it was either a sales call or a wrong number that had pulled him out of his very comfortable position next to Kendall. "Hello?"

"I need to speak to Kendall," a woman with a strong Southern accent demanded.

"Who is this, please?"

"It's Beth."

Web hadn't realized that Kendall had given her friend this number. While he wasn't concerned that the call could be traced since the Shey Groups communications system would encrypt both sides of the conversation and couldn't be traced back to Kendall, he was irritated that she hadn't mentioned giving the number to her friend. "Beth, Kendall's asleep."

"Wake her up. It's an emergency."

At the edge of panic in Beth's voice, Web's irritation vanished. He shook Kendall's shoulder. "Anything I can do to help?"

"I don't know." Beth drew in a loud breath and let it out in a sigh as if trying to gain control of her panic. "Someone tried to kill me."

"Hold on. Kendall needs to hear this, too. I'm putting you on the speakerphone." Web made sure she was awake, took a moment to enjoy the tender look in her eyes when she first saw him before noting the cell phone in his hand. "It's Beth. She thinks someone tried to kill her."

"I don't *think* it." Beth spoke clearly. "I *know* it."

"What happened? Are you okay?" Kendall demanded, her eyes wide, her voice worried.

"After I left you guys at my place, I drove home and spent the night with my parents."

"Are they okay?" Kendall interrupted.

"Everyone is fine." Beth's voice trembled. "But we had a fire at the house. We all got out, but everything my parents owned is gone." Her voice broke. "Everything. Photographs from four generations, my grandmother's antiques, the mementos of a lifetime. All gone."

Kendall swept a lock of hair from her face. "Oh, Beth. I'm so sorry."

Web hardened himself against the loss. While he was sympathetic, he had to go into strategic mode. "You mentioned attempted murder?"

"I'm getting to that," Beth said. "The fire wasn't accidental but definitely arson. We could smell the gasoline fumes as we escaped, and the fire chief confirmed an accelerant had been used. We all figured one of Dad's business enemies had finally caught up with him…until this morning.''

"What happened?" Kendall asked, reaching for Web's hand and holding on tight.

"I headed to work and this truck came out of nowhere and ran me off the road. I would have put it down to an accident but the driver shot at me."

"Oh, my God."

"He shot out the side window in the rear on the passenger's side. Forensics pried the bullet out of the back seat and are running it through their system, but I don't expect they'll find a match to a registered weapon."

"Does anyone have reason to be mad at you?" Web asked. "An ex-husband, ex-lover?"

"No, but I'm a newswoman. I probably have lots of enemies."

"What about Nancy Wilcox?" Kendall asked. "She was furious when your father bought the station and you got the job she'd wanted."

"Nancy moved to California two weeks ago and is anchoring in Sacramento. I doubt she's still jealous of me."

"Have you exposed anyone lately?" Web persisted, trying to discount as many possibilities as he could. "A politician? A crime figure?" Web asked.

"Look, in my job it's possible a television viewer could be angry with me or the station. While there are a lot of wackos out there, we haven't received any threats. Local news has been slow. The only one who might have reason to be mad at me is Franklin."

"Have you seen him?" Kendall asked, and Web

realized by the sharpness in her tone that she now believed Franklin might be capable of murder.

"Franklin called my cell last night. He wanted to know if I'd seen you and asked about the trouble at my condo."

Web swore. "That was supposed to have stayed quiet."

"The attack never made the news. But Franklin's FBI buddies must have caught a whiff of the story. I'm not sure how he knew. The bastard pretended to be all concerned but he was fishing for information. And he wasn't that smooth about it."

"What did you tell him?" Web asked.

"I said I was alone. There was a break-in. That the guy crashed through the window, landed wrong and broke his own neck on impact."

"That was good thinking, Beth," Kendall told her friend.

"Yeah, you think fast on your feet," Web added his admiration.

"Well, I don't think Franklin believed me. He called again today, right after I was run off the road and asked if I'd heard from you. I lied, of course. And when he asked why I'd pulled the story about you being missing from the news, I told him that between the fire and the car accident, I had enough troubles of my own. I know that was lame—but I didn't know what else to say. Sorry."

"Beth, there's no need to apologize. You did well." Kendall turned to Web. "We have got to help her."

"Agreed. Beth, I'm going to call Kincaid and ask him to send one of our people to protect you."

"I'd appreciate it."

"In the meantime, go to the police station and sit in the lobby until someone calls. I'll have our guy identify himself by using the code phrase 'black clouds.' You do whatever he says, okay?"

"Okay."

"Beth?" Kendall's worry clouded her eyes.

"Yeah?"

"I'm sorry I got you into this."

"It's not your fault. It's Franklin's. Somehow, we've got to nail this guy."

"Agreed."

Web let the two women speak while he used his own cell to phone Kincaid and informed his boss of the situation. After he made arrangements with Kincaid, he wasn't surprised to find the women still talking. The talk had turned personal, about him and Kendall. He caught just the tail end of the women's conversation—something about Kendall's confusion about her feelings.

However, once Kendall realized he was listening, she stopped speaking, giving Web the chance to inform them, "Travis Cantral will arrive in Alabama in less than an hour. He's hitching a ride on a military jet out of MacDill Air Force Base. Beth, the guy is ex-military, you can trust him. He has your cell phone number and will call you as soon as he lands—if your batteries are still charged."

"No problem. I always carry a spare." Beth paused. "I'm walking through the front doors of the police station now. "I should be fine. But you stay in touch."

"You, too." Kendall turned off the phone, her gaze thoughtful. "I hate that she's in danger. We have to put a stop to Franklin."

Uh-oh. Web didn't like the determined look on Kendall's face. "Stopping Franklin is not my job. And right now, we have to get out of here."

"Why?"

"Because Franklin's going to monitor Beth's cell. While he can't identify who she spoke to, or listen in on our conversation, he might be able to pinpoint our location. And he's going to wonder who she could have been talking to that could encrypt a call. We're lucky she's a reporter. She could have been conversing with someone from the Pentagon for a story, but Franklin is going to cover his bases. So we have to stay ahead of him."

Kendall wound the sheet around her as she leaped out of bed. "I'll be ready to leave in ten minutes."

"Five would be better."

SINCE KENDALL HAD little to pack, she dressed, brushed her teeth and helped Web with the gear. They moved swiftly to the vehicle, and once they drove from the spa into town, she noted that Web checked the rear mirror frequently, changed lanes often and went around several blocks unnecessarily.

He noted her watching him. "It's just a precaution. I haven't spotted a tail. All the same, we need to change vehicles."

She'd been about to start a conversation, but waited until after he pulled into a used-car lot, haggled, then traded in their vehicle for a late-model BMW. Once they settled the paperwork and transferred their stuff, she'd marshaled her thoughts. "How long have you been assigned to protect me?"

"Until your father finishes his invention or until we catch Franklin, whichever comes first."

"My father has been working on this engine since before I was born. Any estimate on when he expects to be done?"

"Apparently, Kincaid asked him that question and he said genius can't be rushed."

Kendall groaned. "And exactly what is our government doing to catch Franklin?"

"That's classified."

"Great."

"I hope you mean that. I'll be assigned to protect you for a while… I rather like that idea."

And she liked him liking the idea of spending time with her. Only, they couldn't put themselves first. "My best friend's family lost their home and she almost lost her life. Franklin needs to be caught soon."

"We're working on it."

"That's not good enough."

"Look, I know you're upset about Beth. But with Travis on his way to protect her, she'll be fine."

"I do have other friends besides Beth," Kendall pointed out. "Is the Shey Group prepared to guard all of them?"

"We'll do what we can."

Her gut twisted with fear but her determination didn't waver. "I want to go back to Canfield, Web. It's time for me to do something about Franklin."

His tone remained mild but threaded with steel beneath. "Have you forgotten how dangerous he is? That he intended to kidnap you and possibly turn you over to a terrorist organization?"

She snorted. "Like I could forget."

"Look, I know you're impatient for all the espionage to be over and done. Let me touch base with

Kincaid and find out what kind of progress our guys are making. Maybe he can give us an estimate of what time frame we're looking at.''

"Okay." She didn't want to seem unreasonable when Web was trying so hard to placate her. But she'd also picked up on the words *estimate* and *time frame*. "But isn't everything classified?"

"Yeah, but we needn't be specific to find out what stage the operation is in. The difficulty is that Franklin has legitimate reasons to contact the terrorists. We already know he's in touch with them.''

Web phoned Kincaid, asked a few terse questions and hung up with a shake of his head. "Sorry. We don't want to reveal we are on to him until we can put him and his fellow traitors in jail for life. He's careful. And he's good at covering his tracks. Right now, let's hope he still believes you got cold feet and that we're not protecting you.''

Kendall was about to make another suggestion when Web made a sharp right-hand turn. "We've picked up a tail.''

The next hour was tense. Kendall didn't speak. She didn't want to distract Web from his driving. He lost the tail, then carefully circled back and had her write down the driver's tag and phoned it into his home office. She learned that the car was stolen and that Franklin had been seen fifteen minutes earlier at FBI headquarters in Mobile. While he couldn't have been in the car that had been tailing them, the driver might work for him. And that driver could believe he was doing legitimate work—especially if Franklin had lied to him.

Just thinking about the possibilities made her head ache. Worst of all, she realized Franklin may have been checking up on Beth's phones calls to have found them so quickly. When Web circled onto the interstate, she finally asked him, "How much do you think Franklin knows?"

"He's probably on a fishing expedition. Beth's call was suspicious because it was encrypted."

"I don't understand."

"Imagine someone speaking a foreign language. You can't understand the words, but you can pinpoint their location with the right electronics equipment. The encryption would make him curious, so Franklin sent someone to investigate. I doubt he knows you are in this car with me. Now that I've lost them, they'll know they are dealing with a professional."

"That's bad, isn't it?" She sighed. "I shouldn't have given Beth our cell number, but I'm glad I did. It's my fault she's in trouble."

As usual, Web's tone was patient. "First of all, it's not your fault. It's Franklin's—never forget that. Second, giving Beth the number was not a bad idea. But you should have told me."

"Sorry. It won't happen again. I was worried about her, and despite knowing that Franklin is at fault, I still feel responsible. Beth wouldn't be in danger if it wasn't for her association with me. That's why I feel the need to do something."

"Right now, the best thing we can do is to foil Franklin's attempts to find you. That's why we didn't stick with the original plan of a safe house. No one knows where we are, especially the FBI."

Web sounded so certain. And she supposed he was right. His Shey Group had sent someone to protect Beth. What else could she ask for?

Except her life back? And that seemed petty with all that was at stake.

It wasn't as if she didn't enjoy spending time with Web. But it wasn't as if they were on some romantic vacation together. Not when she couldn't call her friends. Not when Beth was in danger. Not when she and Web had to pick up and leave at a moment's notice and hide as if they were fugitives from the law.

She would have suggested that Web take her to the same secret facility as her father, but he needed to complete his work and she doubted the man who hadn't made one effort to ever speak to his daughter would appreciate her showing up now. Kendall had never been so uncertain in her life. Always she'd had a goal, whether it was finishing her education, earning enough money to pay her bills or taking care of her mom, she'd gotten up in the morning knowing what she had to do that day. Now she felt as though she was drifting. And with no idea what the day would bring, uncertainties plagued her.

She liked Web. Already she felt as though she knew what made him tick much better than she'd ever known Franklin. Web had let her inside. He'd shared parts of his past, told her about his family, his work, his boss. She liked that he didn't play games. She could count on Web to protect her, to hold her, to make love to her. Steady, solid, sensual, he would be there for her.

But she'd been just as certain about Franklin. And look how badly that decision had turned out. Spending so much continuous time with Web may have scrambled her normal caution over jumping into a relationship, but she didn't regret making love with

Web. In fact, she couldn't wait until they could be together again.

With Web she felt as if she could be herself. She didn't have to hide her nature behind expected conventions. She didn't have to be politically correct. She could say what she meant and not worry about his disapproval. Although she hadn't had many serious relationships, she'd dated enough men to know that what she shared with Web was rare and precious. And she didn't want to back away, until she'd decided if being with him was more than a mutual attraction that would lose its magnetism as the newness wore off.

Right now she was still at the giddy stage. Where his every look seemed significant. Where she was still trying to understand where he was coming from. Where she had such an awareness of him that it seemed as if he'd become a part of her. Never before had she felt this intensity with a man. She hadn't known she had that kind of passion inside her.

So spending more time with Web would have appealed to her on every level if Beth hadn't been in danger, and if Kendall didn't feel so uncertain about the future. With her stomach rumbling with hunger, with the moon rising, she had no idea what would happen next. And as much as she trusted Web's judgment, she didn't like being kept in the dark.

"Where are we going?"

"I'm looking for a small bed-and-breakfast. Someplace off the beaten track where we can hide for a few days, pay cash and not cause the townsfolk to notice strangers."

"We could go to Honeymoon Cove and pretend to be newlyweds."

"Honeymoon Cove?"

"It's Alabama's answer to Niagara Falls. A secluded motel around a lake. Canoes. Sailboats. Heart-shaped hot tubs. And I have an idea. After Beth is protected, why don't we have her call Franklin and tell him where I am?"

"What?" The surprise in Web's tone warned her to explain with care.

"Only, I won't be at the location Beth names and then the good guys can swoop in and take him."

"Franklin can claim he has every right to look for his missing fiancé."

"But suppose he doesn't just try to talk to me."

"You want to set a trap?"

"Yes."

Web shook his head. "If Franklin doesn't do anything violent, we'll have no reason to arrest him. Then he'll become suspicious and possibly suspend his activities until the heat is off and we won't catch his associates." Web smoothly switched lanes. "Besides, I don't like the idea of using you for bait—even when I know you're safe."

"According to you, Franklin's already coming after me whether we set a trap or not. At least this way, we can be prepared for his arrival."

"And what would you have Beth tell him?"

Although she suspected Web was probably continuing this conversation for the sole purpose of discouraging her, she couldn't give up on the idea. "I'd have Beth say that I got cold feet before the wedding. That I've been crying my eyes out ever since I ran. And that I don't have the courage to tell him that running away was the biggest mistake of my life."

"I appreciate the idea, but our government has been investigating Franklin for some time. They don't just want him. They want him to reveal his contacts both up and down the ladder. They want to know which people inside the FBI may be helping him and which are innocent. They might even want to infiltrate the terrorist organization."

Kendall sighed. "This sounds like it could take years."

"Probably weeks. Maybe a month or two."

"And I'm supposed to put my life on hold?" Kendall leaned back against the car seat. "I suppose that sounds selfish, but I spent my childhood waiting for my dad to contact me. I put off college to take care of my mom. I don't want to wait. I don't want to waste one day, never mind weeks. Watching my mom waste away taught me that our days could be more limited than we think. And while I enjoy our time together, running and looking over our shoulders is no way to live."

"The most difficult part of my job is always the waiting. Waiting to hear the details of the mission. Waiting for the right moment to carry it out. Waiting to go home again." With that, they drove on in silence.

An hour later she gazed at the hotel. Long, low, with private balconies on every lakefront room, the resort should have felt welcoming. Lovers strolled hand in hand along the lake. Several couples made use of canoes, rowboats and the dock. Others gathered around the pool where someone strummed a guitar. Yet she didn't feel as if she belonged here. She wasn't one of those happy, mellow souls on vacation. She was hiding.

"How do you get yourself through the waiting?"

"I read, talk, play solitaire. Rarely has the waiting been as pleasant as the time I've been with you." His voice was smooth, rich and perhaps a bit hurt.

"Web, it's not you that I want to get away from. You've been wonderful. It's just that I'm not accustomed to sleeping in a different bed every night. Or waking up wondering where I'll be going that day or who will be coming after me. I don't mind planned adventure. But not knowing what's going to happen from one minute to the next isn't exciting. It's wearing me down. Making me cranky and...hungry."

He flashed a grin at her. "I'm sure they have a dining room here. Why don't we eat before we check into the room?"

"Sounds good." She knew he didn't like to leave his equipment untended in the locked hotel room where so many people had access.

"And as for the crankiness—" he winked at her "—if you give me a chance, I'll see what I can do about that later."

The dining room was surprisingly crowded. However, they didn't have to wait for a table. Web had asked for a secluded spot near a rear exit with his back to the wall and where he could face the room. She'd noted how carefully he chose their position, as if it might be a life-and-death decision, yet he did so with the casual ease of someone who made such choices automatically.

The candlelit room and the white linen tablecloths set with gleaming silver, delicate crystal and china helped settle her nerves. The impeccable service and the string quartet lent a romantic mood to the room, as did the fire blazing in the fireplace.

She ordered a house salad and veal picata in lemon-butter sauce with capers, and Web ordered a steak. They split a bottle of wine, and after the delicious meal, she was feeling relaxed and ready for some Mississippi mud pie. Web had set his phone to vibrate so the ring wouldn't disturb other diners, but from the moment he reached into his pocket and pulled out the phone, her nerves grew ragged.

As if knowing her fear about Beth, he checked the caller ID. "It's Kincaid," he told her, turning his attention to the phone.

Web's expression didn't change. His boss might have been relaying the weather, and yet the man didn't call just to chat. She prayed for good news. That Franklin had been cleared or caught. That Beth and she could go back to their normal lives. That her father had completed his invention, turned it over to the government or car companies. Once he finished and the technology was out in the open, no terrorist organization would bother with Kendall, her friend or her father. They'd all be safe.

So she watched Web's face. The expression in his eyes didn't change. His muscles didn't tense. And yet she sensed if the news had been good, he would have reached out and taken her hand, his mouth would have softened, his eyes would have gleamed in satisfaction.

"How long do we have?" Web asked Kincaid.

That didn't sound good. Her heart skittered and her mouth went dry.

What was going on? Were they going to spend the night? Or leave? Despite Web's efforts to lose the tail, had they been followed without his knowledge?

She told herself to stay calm. To breathe. Web could be discussing his next assignment. He could be discussing how long until her father completed his invention. Or how long until Travis reached Beth.

Web snapped shut his cell phone, signaled the waiter and asked for their bill. Lowering his voice, he gave her the bad news. ''Someone in this restaurant recognized you from Beth's publicity. They called the FBI.''

Even as she marveled at Kincaid's information network, her heart thudded up her throat. ''Franklin knows we're here?''

Chapter Ten

"Kincaid estimates we have a thirty-minute head start, maybe only ten, if Franklin can commandeer a chopper," Web told her as they headed back to their vehicle. "Don't look around. Gaze at me as if you know how much I want to kiss you."

She wanted to run, but Web kept their pace steady and even, so as not to attract attention. She was sure everyone was staring at them, but he'd asked her to look at him as if she couldn't take her eyes off his. Normally having an excuse to look at him wouldn't have been a problem. She enjoyed the strength in Web's face, the intelligence in his eyes, the humor so often revealed in his upturned lips. But not with the FBI about to show up. Not when she wasn't ready to confront Franklin.

Web took extra time to stop at the front desk, pretending they would check into their room as he paid for three nights and asked directions to a hiking path, leaving a false trail if anyone asked. But when Franklin and his men checked their room and found it empty, they'd search for their vehicle, and when they failed to find it, they'd suspect she'd left.

Web led her straight to their car. He grabbed the

backpack with cash, a gun, a knife and several cell phones. Perhaps Web meant to leave the vehicle behind, too. But he gestured for her to get in.

''We'll park down by the lake.'' He drove to the far end of the crowded parking lot, slowly bumped their way over a curb, and half hid the vehicle behind some bushes. ''Wait here.''

Web removed a sack of equipment from the rear passenger seat and tossed it into the lake where it sank from sight. Next he untied one of the rowboats and shoved it into the lake, before returning to her and hefting the pack onto his back. ''Let's hope the boat drifts to the other side.''

''Where are we going?'' she asked.

''Kincaid said if we head due north, he'll have someone meet us.''

''Who?''

''I don't know. Kincaid has thousands of contacts in the police, CIA and military. Sometimes it's a friend of a friend of someone who owes him a favor. Sometimes the contact is simply hired to do the job. Whoever meets us will be someone who keeps his mouth shut and who will identify himself by one red and one green pen in his front pocket.'' Web handed her a cell phone and pointed to a narrow path that forked to the right. ''You go on ahead. I want to wipe the car clean. I'll catch up within half an hour.''

She didn't like the idea of leaving him. She didn't want to go on alone. And yet she didn't want to waste time arguing. Delays meant that Franklin had a better shot at catching up with them. Still, she took time to fling herself into Web's arms and plant a kiss on his welcoming lips before heading up the path alone.

Without Web beside her, she started at every crackle in the brush, at each darting squirrel, chirping frog and cooing bird. While she wasn't a city girl and had grown up in the suburbs, this part of Alabama was almost as remote as the area where the chopper had gone down. At least the path was well marked and she had no fear of becoming lost in the dark.

To lift her spirits, she counted her blessings. She wasn't cold, hungry or wet. She wore comfortable hiking shoes, jeans and a jacket. She had a cell phone if she needed to call for help. She wasn't sick, tired or even sore.

So why did she feel so down?

The tension was getting to her. The constant running and looking over her shoulder was stressing her out. And without Web there to buffer her from her true feelings and to distract her with interesting conversation, she knew she couldn't take much more of this. She'd heard of people who had been on the run for decades and then turned themselves in to the law, knowing they would face severe consequences. Now she knew why.

She needed to go on with her life. She needed to make plans for her future. But that kind of normalcy was impossible until either her father finished his invention or the government caught Franklin and his cohorts. She could do nothing to speed up her father's progress. And Web hadn't liked her plan to catch Franklin. Perhaps she could think up another.

Kendall strode quickly down the path at a fast walk. She'd been thinking so hard that she stopped startling at the sounds from the woods, and it took a moment for her to identify Web's evenly paced running footsteps until he came alongside her. "Everything okay?"

"I suppose."

"What's wrong?" he asked, his tone a sharp whisper as he scanned ahead as if expecting danger to pop out of the trees and confront them.

"The food in my fridge is rotting. My car payment is overdue. I haven't paid my electric bill and my credit—"

"I'll have Kincaid take care of it."

"Thanks…"

"But," he pressed, "what else?"

"Web, living on the run like this is wearing me down," she admitted. Although she hated to complain, she didn't think he had a clue why she was upset.

"We'll go far away. Somewhere we can settle for a while. How does Maine or the Caribbean sound?"

"They sound great for a vacation, but I can't relax when I'm always expecting something bad to happen. I want to go home. I want my life back. I need this to be over."

Web placed an arm around her shoulders and hugged her. "Hang in there. We're going to be fine."

Easy for him to say. His life wasn't being disrupted. Being on the move all the time *was* his life. And while she didn't mean to be ungrateful, if she could do something to help, she wanted the opportunity.

"Web, I have another idea how to make this all end sooner."

She knew he wouldn't laugh or make a dismissing remark, but she didn't expect him to sound so curious. "Tell me," he encouraged her.

"If I understood you correctly, our government needs to catch Franklin in the act of plotting terrorism or committing a treasonous act?"

"Yes."

"What if I go back to Franklin—"

"No. You'd be in too much danger," Web insisted, his tone hard.

"I'm already in danger." She squeezed Web's hand. "Hear me out, please."

"Okay," he agreed, but his tone didn't soften.

"If Franklin's still looking for me, he's hoping to talk me into changing my mind about marrying him. He wants to carry out his original plan, right?"

"Maybe," Web conceded.

"So we let him. I'll go back and tell Franklin that I got cold feet right before the wedding. That I ran away for a few days to think things over and have realized I made a huge mistake. I'll tell him how much I love him and ask his forgiveness."

"And then?" Web's tone remained hard but interested.

"If I go back to him, won't he have to make plans? Talk to his cohorts and contact the terrorists? You'll be watching every move he makes. You'll be able to catch him."

"You want me to let you go to him?" Web shook his head. "You'd have to meet alone with Franklin. Probably several times."

"So? He doesn't want to kill me. I'm of no use to him dead."

''We can't send you in with a wire. He's too smart for that.''

''Don't you have other kinds of listening devices? Couldn't you bug the room ahead of time?'' She let her enthusiasm enter her tone. ''Please, Web. I don't want to keep running for months and months. I want to catch him and move on with my life.''

''And my spiriting you away to some vacation spot won't satisfy you?'' Web's tone sounded sad, disappointed.

''This isn't just about us. Besides, I'm not sure what to think about us. But I can't evaluate my feelings when we're on the run. When the only person I see and talk to is you. When I'm scared and anxious. This isn't the real world. It's more like a romantic thriller than my life. And that may be the kind of world where you're comfortable, but no matter how terrific the locale, I'm not comfortable hiding out.''

Web removed his hand from her shoulder. His words, so controlled, so contained, revealed to her more than a shout just how much she'd hurt him. ''So what am I to you? Someone you filled up the hours with when no one else was available? Someone you used to chase away your fears?''

''That's not fair.'' She stopped walking but he didn't wait for her, giving her his back. Hurrying to catch up, she tried to explain after having made such a mess of things. ''My point is that until my life returns to normal, I won't know how I feel. I obviously made a huge mistake thinking I loved Franklin, and part of that was due to grieving over the loss of my mother. How do I know that what I feel for you isn't due to forced proximity, danger and that my life is in your hands?''

"It wasn't just your life in my hands. I don't recall you complaining when I—"

"Don't. Don't say something that we'll both regret." She tugged on his shoulder and he reluctantly turned around. "Web, I want a real chance for us to spend more time together. Time where we can relax, where a phone call won't send us running into the woods in the middle of the night to meet some stranger who will take us someplace I've never been before. I'm not trying to negate what we have together."

"And what do we have together?" he challenged her.

"That's what I want to find out. And I can't trust my feelings while I'm so off-kilter, so emotionally charged or wrung out, so worried over Beth that I don't know if I'm thinking straight."

"Maybe you're thinking too much."

He reached for her and she didn't resist. His arms around her felt good and she tipped up her head, her lips automatically searching for his. But instead of kissing her as she expected, he jerked back. "You wanted me to kiss you, don't deny it."

"Of course I want you to kiss me. Why would I deny it?"

"Hell, woman, you are sending me so many mixed signals I'm not sure what to think."

WHEN KENDALL DIDN'T RESPOND, they both began to walk through the woods again. Unlike their journey through the swamp, the path was even beneath their feet, the route clear. A pleasant breeze kept mosquitoes at bay, and a crescent moon overhead lit the way.

Shoving his confusion about Kendall from his mind, Web tried to think rationally about her suggestion. However, the idea of her going back to Franklin rankled Web on several levels. First, it was dangerous. She wasn't a trained operative and predicting Franklin's moves might be tricky. Second, several government agencies would have to be brought in and that upped the chances of a leak as well as increasing the danger. Third, Web didn't like the idea of her going back and spending time with the man she'd almost married.

He hadn't had enough time with her yet to feel certain that she preferred him to the traitor. While he told himself this wasn't jealousy but prudent behavior, in truth, he wasn't so sure. The idea of her spending time with Franklin irritated the hell out of him, and Web told himself it was because he was almost certain Kincaid would approve of Kendall's suggestion. Kincaid usually favored action over reaction and would see the merit in her idea of forcing Franklin's hand.

Kendall had proposed a scenario that any intelligence agent would appreciate, yet she couldn't comprehend the kind of danger she might be placing herself in. These people didn't value life the way Americans did. Terrorists often found honor in dying for their causes and considered any form of negotiation a weakness. With Kendall's father's invention, the West would eventually become independent of the oil from the Mid East—oil that had made that area of the world incredibly wealthy and raised those countries' levels of importance politically and economically.

Her father's invention would alter the balance of world power in favor of the United States. From a Middle-Eastern point of view, their very survival could depend upon squashing the invention and anyone who stood in their way. With her father protected within the bowels of a secret underground military facility, Kendall had become a pawn in a power game where the stakes were billions of dollars.

Even if the Shey Group stopped Franklin, his associates and the terrorists he worked with, unless they captured the leaders behind the scheme, Kendall would not be safe. But there was no better way to take the group down than by using her as bait. In many respects, she'd evaluated her situation with an accuracy that astonished Web, and she was correct that whether she posed as bait or not, she would still be in danger.

If they sent her to Franklin, she would have to go in with no training. It would take years to teach her hand-to-hand fighting, weeks more to handle a gun with the proficiency needed to take out experts. And the nature of what would be required would mean she'd have to go alone.

Damn.

Web didn't like it. So many things could go wrong. She could easily end up injured or hurt. He didn't want to lose her. She'd become important to him. He enjoyed spending time with her. Adored kissing and making love to her. And he wanted time to get to know her much better.

That she'd made the suggestion to go to Franklin

proved to Web that she had courage. Since they'd met, she'd repeatedly proven she thought fast on her feet and could improvise when necessary. However, she'd also warned him that looking over her shoulder and running was wearing her down.

The path narrowed and forced them to walk single file, then once again it widened. He waited until she came up beside him before speaking what was on his mind.

"If you think the stress level is high now, it's going to escalate tenfold if we allow you to approach Franklin. Before I contact Kincaid, I want to know if you're certain this is what you want to do."

"I don't want to go on as we have been. And you told me waiting was the hard part. I want the waiting to be over. Surely you understand that?"

"We won't be able to put someone inside the room with you and Franklin. We probably can't risk bugging it, either," he explained. "Franklin has access to all the same equipment we do. What we can bug, he can debug."

"I understand. But I also know that he doesn't intend to hurt me."

Web's gut churned. Franklin would keep her safe for as long as she was useful to him—and not one moment longer. "Don't kid yourself. If he intends to turn you over to terrorists, we can't guarantee your safety."

"I know. But with my help, there's a much better chance of stopping him and getting all of his people. Right?"

"Yeah. And once you go back to him, he may be so wary of blowing his cover that he does nothing at all—except set you up for someone else to take.

While we believe that Nate crashed the chopper and that Franklin has no idea what happened to you, we may never be certain.''

"But you'll be monitoring him and watching over me, right?" she insisted, as if not the least bit worried whether they could protect her. Either she had too much faith in him or she was ignorant of how complicated things could become.

"We'll watch, yes. But from a distance. If we come in too close, we risk him catching on to what we're doing. And this is all hypothetical—until I speak to Kincaid."

"You don't like my idea, do you?" she asked.

Web was saved from having to answer as the path ended at a dirt road. Up ahead a man in a late-model four-wheel-drive pickup truck with a trailer attached to a hitch appeared to be waiting for them.

Web approached and the man lit a cigarette. His face was wrinkled, his hair and beard were long and gray, and in his front pocket he had two pens, one green, the other red.

"Nice night for a ride." Web referred to the motorcycle on the trailer. As of yet, he wasn't sure if he was supposed to drive out in the truck or on the bike. He could handle either and Kincaid knew that from his file. However, when Web leaned slightly forward, he saw two helmets on the front seat.

The old man handed them to him, then exited the truck. "There's a map and gear packed in the saddlebags. The fuel tank is topped off." He unlocked the trailer, hopped into the truck's bed and rolled the bike to the dirt road. "She's all yours."

"Thanks. Appreciate the help."

The man tipped his cap, flicked his cigarette butt

to the road, ground it out with the heel of his boot, kicked dirt over it, then ground it out some more. When he bent, retrieved the butt and placed it back into his pocket, Web suspected the guy was ex-CIA. He might appear to be an old hippie, but his eyes were sharp and he surveyed the woods with a wary eye.

"There's two ways out of here if you stay on the road." He jerked his thumb. "That'll take you out of state and into Mississippi." He jerked his thumb at an angle. "That way goes upstate. If I didn't want anyone to find me, I'd ride over the hills. Lots of open farmland. A man could get himself real lost out here in a hurry."

"Thanks." Web handed Kendall her helmet. He placed the other over his head and snapped down the clear visor. He didn't say which way he intended to go and the man didn't ask. Instead the guy got back into his truck and headed out.

Web didn't climb onto the cycle until the truck's engine was just a hum in the distance. Although he suspected the man no more wanted to know his direction than Web wanted to have him know it, Web was careful out of habit. If he'd intended to keep hiding, he would have headed for the hills, but he wanted to talk to Kincaid about sending Kendall back to Franklin.

If Kincaid approved her idea, he would have to take her home. And the idea made his heart heavy, his nerves ragged.

WEB STEERED THE MOTORCYCLE back toward Canfield with trepidation that he tried to ignore. The idea of losing Kendall to Franklin sucked. But instead of dwelling on the negative, he forced positives into his mind.

He concentrated on the feel and freedom of cutting through the wind, of Kendall's hands around his waist. This could very well be their last night alone together, and he didn't want to spoil it with his doubts. He was determined to make the most of what they did have and enjoy every minute with Kendall and ensure she enjoyed him, too.

It was after midnight when he pulled into a bed-and-breakfast about fifty miles north of Canfield. The private room with a canopy king-size bed lent a romantic air to the decor and he hurried through necessary business.

While Kendall showered, Web called Kincaid with her plan. Just as Web had suspected, Kincaid saw the merit of her idea and okayed it on the spot. He also informed Web that Franklin had driven up to the Honeymoon Hotel after the witness had reported seeing Kendall there. His FBI team had found their abandoned vehicle and little else. So Franklin couldn't know for certain whether or not Kendall had been there. Then Kincaid had assured Web he'd have a team in place to monitor and keep her safe by morning when they agreed she should phone Franklin. The two men went over details and agreed to touch base again before putting the plan into play the next day.

With business done, Web entered the shower to find Kendall with a towel wrapped around her, staring into the mirror as if she'd never seen herself before. Coming up behind her, he placed a hand on her shoulders and kneaded tight muscles. "You okay?"

"I'm ready for this to be over." She leaned back and let out a soft moan of appreciation as he massaged her.

"Anxious to be rid of me?" he teased.

"You know better."

But did he? All he knew was that in the morning she was leaving him to return to Franklin, and he didn't like it one little bit. Knowing that she and Franklin had never made love only helped somewhat. Just the idea of her being in the traitor's presence annoyed Web, making him realize that he'd come to care for Kendall more than he'd thought possible within such a short span of time.

Wanting to show her how much she meant to him, he reached for her comb, threaded it through her hair and worked out the tangles. He took his time, and when the task was done, he reached for the hair dryer, but she took it from him with a shaky smile. "I'll dry while you shower."

Web gave up the blow-dryer, stepped into the shower, shampooed, soaped and shaved. When he stepped out again, he half expected her to be in bed, asleep. So when he saw her sitting on the bed, wrapped only in a towel, slowly applying lotion to her arms, his eyes widened with pleasure. Kendall had the long, graceful limbs of a ballet dancer. Toned, strong, yet utterly feminine, she captivated him as she poured body lotion into her palm and then smoothed it over her shoulder.

With a towel wrapped around his hips, he went over to her. She smelled of shampoo, toothpaste and the vanilla scent of lotion. "Can I do your back?"

"Sure." Her gaze locked with his, igniting a fire in his gut as she offered him the lotion. She turned onto her stomach, her golden hair fanning across the pillow, and the towel splitting open at her side, taunting him with a peek of golden skin.

With one tug he pulled away the towel and marveled at the perfection of her back, the soft curve of her shoulders, the smoothness of her delicate waist and the wonderful roundness of her bottom. Like a sensual feast spread out before him, she was tempting, tantalizing and, oh-so touchable that his mouth watered. Sitting beside her on the bed, he decided that before he was done, she would be wanting him as much as he wanted her.

"Web?" Her voice was low and husky, inviting.

"Yeah?"

"Aren't you going to touch me?"

"There's so many enticing places that I'm deciding where to start." He blew a breath of air behind her ear and onto her neck.

At his attention, the tiny hairs on her nape stood on end. "Oh...my."

He blew air down her spine and over her bottom and watched her quiver in anticipation of his touch. "So do you have a preference?"

"Huh?" Her voice was tight yet dreamy, as if she was having difficulty following the conversation.

"A preference where I should begin?"

She squirmed a little, then looked over her shoulder at him, her eyes glazed with desire. "Touch me, Web. Anywhere you want."

He chuckled. "Now that's an invitation I intend to accept." Web turned the lotion upside down and gently squeezed out a few drops at a time. The lotion rained on her neck and shoulders, along her spine and the dimples at her hips. He shook out more lo-

tion and let it dribble over her bottom, the insides
of her thighs, the backs of her knees and the soles
of her feet.

He had yet to touch her, but her breath grew ragged, and all his blood seemed to surge south. The
pulse at her throat throbbed, and his fingers tingled
with the urge to smooth the lotion over her sleekly
tanned skin. When he placed his hands so they
spanned her waist, a muscle leaped beneath his
palm. And when he skimmed his hands up her sides
and allowed his fingertips to coast the rims of her
breasts, she released a long, low sigh of appreciation.

The muscles in her back were taut from tension
and the long motorcycle ride. But he wasn't as interested in easing sore muscles as he was in creating
a very different kind of stress.

He wanted her thinking about where and how he'd
touch her next. He wanted her wanting him so much
that she couldn't hold still, wanting him so much
that she couldn't resist turning over and reaching for
him, wanting him so much that she'd never forget
what they had together.

He intended to lead her right to the edge, again
and again, before he allowed her to take them both
over. So as much as he wanted her right this moment, he held back to give them both more pleasure.
If they were to have only this last night together, he
wanted it to be one they would remember for the
rest of their lives. And hopefully someday she'd understand exactly how much she meant to him. While
she wasn't yet ready to hear his words, he could
show her how he felt about her as he worshipped
her body.

Web slathered lotion all over her back, her bottom

and her legs until her skin was slick, the oil gleaming over every inch of her. Then slowly, beginning with her feet, he smoothed the lotion into her skin, letting her soak up the heat of his hands, the moisture of the lotion and most of all the sensuality of his touch.

When her fingers clenched and unclenched at her sides, he figured that his assault on her senses was attaining the desired results and applied himself with an eagerness that shook him. Determined to delay her pleasure, he realized his tactic was a two-edged sword, because she wasn't the only one who had to hold back or who was suffering from the escalating heat. For both of them, touching her was sweet torture.

"Web."

"Yeah?"

"I want to turn over now."

"And I want you to, but not yet."

"But—" She raised up on one elbow and peered over at him, her lips pouting with impatience.

At her movement, one knee bent and her thighs parted a bit more. Web slipped his hand between her legs.

"Oh," she murmured, "you don't play fair."

"Is that a complaint?" he asked, teasing her moist folds.

"Yes, damn you." She wriggled. "Are you deliberately trying to make me insane?"

"Hey, if you can talk that well, I must not be doing my job correctly."

She giggled. "There's a correct way to do what you're doing right now?"

"Of course there is." And he proceeded to show her.

Chapter Eleven

Web's magical hands and clever fingers had Kendall awash in fiery sensations that left her breathless. With every cell in her body demanding more of his touch, holding still while he applied lotion to her heated skin was an exercise in futility. She'd never known lovemaking could be so erotic or playful or fun. Or that she could be so needy for more.

With her senses responding to Web like a finely tuned piano, her blood sang with joy, her heart beat to his melody. She'd never felt so alive or natural. Being with him held a rightness that overwhelmed her usual practical self. Once again she found herself yielding to the pleasure of his touch and his giving nature.

"When…do I get…to put the lotion…on you?" she asked as heat singed a blaze straight to her core.

"Later."

His fingers moved faster, making speech difficult. "How much…later?"

"After we make love."

"That's not…ah…I can't think when you…"

"Don't think, babe. Tell me how you feel."

"Hot."

"What else?"

"Ragged. On edge."

"Tell me." He withdrew his hand from between her legs and kissed her shoulder.

"I feel like a train about to run off the track. Like a sky diver about to leap into space. You've...left me hanging on by a thread." She turned from her stomach to her back, grabbed him and pulled him close for a long, thorough kiss.

Even as her lips claimed his, even as she sipped desire from his mouth that stoked her to new heights, her fingers clenched him with the beginnings of desperation. "Web, make love to me."

"I will." He reached for the lotion, a gleam of hunger in his eyes, a touch of deviltry on his mouth. Then he flicked droplets of lotion over her neck, her chest, her stomach.

A spurt of heat fired between her thighs as she realized that he meant to spread the lotion over this side of her, too. "But I want you now," she complained.

He took her nipple between his teeth, worked his tongue over the sensitive nub, holding her exactly where he wanted her. His hand closed over her other breast, spreading the lotion, licking circles of heat until her back arched, and soft uncontrollable moans of pleasure danced up her throat.

When she could take no more, she tried to roll him to his back, but he wouldn't budge. Instead he raised his head, looked straight into her eyes, his own expression both fierce and tender. "I love you, Kendall."

She raised her hands to either side of his face. "Then make love to me."

He shook his head. "You aren't listening to my words or your own heart."

"Damn, you, Web. This is no time for a serious conversation. I can't think… You told me not to think…and now you…" Hot frustration rose up her throat to almost choke her. She knew he had feelings for her but she hadn't realized they were so strong. But she was having so much trouble with her own powerful need for him that she couldn't cope with his declaration of love. Her eyes brimmed with unshed tears, and he gathered her into his arms as if he'd realized he'd pushed her too far.

"It's okay. There's no rush. I'll give you all the time in the world." He planted kisses on her forehead, her nose, her cheeks, her chin, suffusing her with a different kind of need.

She'd seen Web's gentleness, his ferocity, his compassion and his tenderness. But until this moment she hadn't seen his vulnerability. When he'd told her, "I love you," he expected some other response than her holding back tears.

But she couldn't give him the words he wanted to hear. She didn't know how she felt, didn't trust her own judgment. And with her blood surging, she only knew that the intensity of her emotions scared her. She could give him that at least.

"Web, I've never felt like this about anyone before and I'm frightened."

"Of me?" He smoothed back her hair, his eyes puzzled.

"Of us. When I'm with you, I don't feel as if I'm in my right mind. My senses are off-kilter. And I want you to hold me so badly that if you let go, I'd be lost."

"I won't let go," he promised.

She knew he wouldn't. And that she could have such an effect on him scared her as much as it empowered her. "Hold me, Web."

He cradled her against his chest, rocking her, soothing her and at the same time, the friction of her oiled skin against his chest was stoking her up all over again. Only this time the passion wasn't hers alone. She could feel his erection pressing against her and opened her legs, but Web still wasn't in a hurry. In fact, she could have sworn from the gleam in his eyes that he fully intended to follow through on his initial plan of driving her wild.

However, with her flesh aching for more of his wondrous touches, she couldn't seem to think of a way to change his mind. And she no longer knew if she wanted to. There was something erotic about giving up total control to him. Of simply experiencing all he had to give.

And she found lovemaking with Web incredibly exciting because she hadn't known she could feel so much, want so much, need so much. When he'd explored her face and neck and slathered lotion over her stomach and legs, when he finally came back to her center and buried himself in her heat, the sweetness of the moment burst in her mind like sunshine.

And afterward, as they lay together in the sheets, their legs entwined, she still didn't want to let go. Together, they had found a special place, created an exclusive haven from the outside world that would intrude all too soon.

But for now, cocooned in warmth, she clung to him, napped and awakened to find him watching her with a sleepy tenderness that melted her heart. Not wanting to spoil the moment with words, she reached for the bottle of lotion, pleased to find he'd left enough for another bout of lovemaking.

Because this time she wanted to be the one to drive him to the brink. She wanted to be the one to explore every muscular inch of him. She wanted to be the one who gave him a special night to remember.

And when the sun first spread pink fingers of dawn across the morning sky, Kendall awakened energized. And ready to face what must be done. Knowing that Web would be with her in spirit and covering her back, she was sure she was up to taking on Franklin. Web's strength gave her the courage to believe she could do what was needed.

As Web made final plans with Kincaid, she realized that she'd been wrong. Web's strength hadn't lent her courage. His strength had allowed her to tap into what had always been inside her. Web had given her so much. And no matter what happened between them she would always be thankful for his showing her what kind of woman she was.

DURING THE DRIVE BACK HOME, Web drilled her on procedure. She listened to his instructions, wondering if his lecture was more for his sake than hers. While she'd try to follow his directions and meet Franklin in public places or at her home where Web's team had bugged the place, if Franklin were suspicious, and he would be, he'd have his own agenda. She would attempt to follow Web's rules, but if Franklin suddenly decided to take her for a walk or ask her over for dinner at his place, she couldn't refuse every time.

Web dropped her off around the corner from the tiny home she'd inherited from her mother. Despite Web's having told her that what the Shey Group could bug, Franklin could debug, Kincaid had assured them his people had the latest in electronic equipment that not even the FBI could detect. The Shey Group had already placed those highly advanced electronic listening devices in every room except her bathroom, and they would monitor her phone line 24/7 through the FBI tap that Franklin already had in place. In addition, Web and Kincaid had provided a cover story for her that would hold up to FBI scrutiny.

Kendall's next-door neighbor on her north side, Mr. Knox, had been encouraged to take a vacation, and from his home, the Shey Group had set up surveillance. Help, should she need it, was simply a shout away. However, unless her life was in immediate danger she was not supposed to call Web, which would blow their carefully laid plans. Kendall would have to trust Web and his people to keep her safe, even if Franklin tried to force her out of town.

As she walked up the driveway, apprehension battled with relief at being home. The frivolous dolphin-shaped mailbox, the green lawn and the familiar rhododendron and the sweeping oak tree that shaded the entire front yard welcomed her with their familiarity. The ,nine-hundred-square-foot brick house might be tiny but it was comfortable. The front door opened into a living area of brown carpeting, paneled walls and a comfortable burnt orange couch. The living and kitchen areas were connected and she headed straight for the phone that hung on the wall by the cozy dining area.

She dialed Franklin's cell phone and swallowed hard as she waited for him to pick up. Her choice would have been to get settled, but Web had insisted that she call Franklin immediately upon arriving, before he found her.

"Special Agent Whitelaw," Franklin answered, his voice sounding irritated and crisp. As usual, he probably hadn't checked his caller ID or he wouldn't have answered the phone in such a businesslike manner.

"Franklin, it's Kendall."

"Kendall?" Franklin's voice was odd, excited as if he didn't quite believe it was really her. "Where are you? Are you okay?"

"I'm home. Could you come by? We need to talk."

"Where have you been?" he demanded. "Why didn't you show up at our wedding?"

"That's why we need to talk." She wondered if he'd always been so cold. There was no *I've missed you*. No *I'm so glad you're alive*. No *I was worried about you*.

"It's the middle of the morning. Why don't you come to my office?"

"We need to talk by ourselves."

"Are you in trouble?"

"I don't want to do this over the phone or in front of your colleagues. Please, Franklin. Can't you take an early lunch?"

"You've never offered to make me lunch before."

Was that suspicion in his tone?

"I was actually thinking you could pick something up on the way. But I can heat up soup and crackers if you prefer.''

Why were they talking about food? Her stomach was in a hundred knots. She wouldn't be able to swallow water, never mind soup or crackers. Web had warned her that fooling Franklin would be emotionally difficult, but she hadn't really understood until now. Web had told her that sticking to the truth was always the easiest and best way to act and she held on to that. If cold feet had been the reason that she'd run from her wedding and she'd had to return to face her potential groom, no doubt she would be nervous. She'd wonder if he would forgive her. Wonder if they'd get back together. So nerves were natural under the real circumstances or the fake ones.

However, she didn't just have to deal with Franklin. Web was next door, listening to every word. She had to wonder what he thought of Franklin's coldness and what kind of woman she'd been to not only put up with the man but to have been ready to marry him. Talk about complicated. Her simple life had suddenly multiplied in complexity, and the beginnings of a headache started to come on.

"Fine," Franklin agreed. "I'll be there in thirty minutes. And I'll need some answers."

It would take him only half that amount of time to drive over. Did he have things on his desk to clear up so he could leave work for the entire day? Or was he notifying his fellow cohorts that she was alive and back in town where he could once again try to manipulate her?

She reminded herself that the Shey Group would monitor Franklin's every phone call, his every conversation. The entire point of her pretending to come back to him was to get him to act. She had to be patient. The operation would take time to unfold. This conversation would be the first of many. And if Franklin was indeed guilty of treason, she didn't have to worry over his forgiveness. He would appear cordial and concerned because his role required him to let her work her way back into his good graces.

She wished she could talk to Web over a radio or walkie-talkie, but he'd told her that kind of communication could be too easily monitored. She'd have to wait to hear his steadying voice until after Franklin left and Web could come over under cover of darkness.

In the meantime she poured herself a glass of water and swallowed two aspirin. To distract herself, she paid her bills and had just begun to throw away some rotting fruit and vegetables when Franklin squealed to a stop in her driveway. He might have appeared to have driven over quickly, but according to her grandfather clock, he'd taken thirty-five minutes.

Kendall rinsed her shaking hands in the sink, dried them on a dish towel and met Franklin at the door. Taller than Web, but with half of Web's musculature, Franklin was slender, his hair damp as if he'd stopped and taken a quick shower. She opened the door and stepped back, wondering if she should just throw herself into his arms. The thought of Web watching from next door stopped her as much as the fact that she and Franklin had had such a reserved relationship that such an action would have seemed desperate to him. And very possibly unwanted.

Kendall wanted to appear thoughtful and reasonable, not desperate, and was pleased when her voice came out sounding almost normal. "Come in."

Franklin stepped inside with his usual arrogance. It wasn't as if he looked down snobbishly at her modest home, but as if he didn't deign to notice the comfortable if shabby furnishings. "I was worried sick about you. I've missed you. Where the hell have you been?"

The first two lines sounded rehearsed. Although he'd obviously tried to put feeling into his words, they seemed forced and insincere now that she knew what to look for. Compared to Web's genuine warmth, Franklin's tepid voice left her cold and so glad that she hadn't married him and made the biggest mistake of her life.

On the other hand, his angry demand about her whereabouts sounded real enough. While his damp brunette hair was neatly combed and he projected concern, she wondered if his brown eyes had always been so sharp, and if his thin lips were always drawn into such a tight line that he appeared to have swallowed something bitter.

"Please have a seat." When he stiffly sat on the sofa, she asked, "Would you like some sweet tea or a cola?"

"What I'd like is an explanation for why you left me standing at the altar, looking like a fool."

This time she heard real embarrassment mixed with a feigned sadness. Sitting in her easy chair opposite the couch, she gave him the cover story Web and she had concocted. "On the way to the wedding, I got scared."

"Why?" This time he revealed bewilderment.

"It was so soon after my mother's death. I was

afraid I was depending on you instead of standing on my own feet. And I wasn't sure I was marrying you for the right reasons.''

''Most brides consider these issues when the man proposes, not on the way to the wedding ceremony.''

''I needed to be certain our marriage was the right thing for me. I had so many doubts. If Mom had been alive she would have reassured me. If Beth had been there she would have told me I was just being silly. But I was alone, and I didn't want to do the wrong thing.''

''Not showing up was the wrong thing.'' Franklin's voice was compassionate. And sour. ''Where did you go? Did you realize the police were looking for you?''

''I had no idea.'' Since the limo driver had been part of the Shey Group operation, he'd disappeared after returning the car, and no one had been able to trace him and question him. His employment records had been faked as well as his address and social security number. Not even Franklin's fellow FBI agents had been able to find him. So this part of her story couldn't be verified. ''I had the limo driver turn around and take me to an old friend of my mother's. She lives about an hour north of Canfield. I stayed with her until I sorted things out.''

''What was her name and address?'' he asked.

Interesting how he was more concerned with verifying her story than what she'd sorted out about their relationship. If she hadn't been certain he was everything Web had claimed—his last question solidified in her mind that Franklin wasn't the upstanding FBI agent he claimed to be.

''What does my location matter?'' she snapped at

him, then put hurt in her tone. "Don't you want to know what I think about us?"

"Of course I do, dear." He leaned over and patted her hand and backtracked. "I just like to get details straight in my mind. And I don't understand why you were so concerned about leaning on me for support. That's what husbands are for."

Oh, he was smooth all right. Once she would have fallen for that kind of line. But now she saw that his words were simply a veneer to cover up his lack of real feeling.

"Then you understand that I also had to get things straight in my mind?" She tossed his own words back in his face but smiled sweetly to take the sting out of her reply.

She suspected he wanted to press her for facts about her whereabouts during her absence but realized how out of character that would be for a man in love. So he swallowed back his curiosity and leaned forward, his eyes intent as if his very future hinged on her.

"And what did you decide about us?" His hands twitched. A muscle in his jaw tightened and he held his breath, the picture of an ardent suitor on pins and needles.

For a brief moment guilt stabbed her. She wasn't a cruel person and to put a man through what she'd put Franklin through was not only heartless but sadistic. What kind of bride-to-be wouldn't have at least phoned to reassure her love that she was safe?

But then Kendall realized that Franklin had never been worried about her—only that her disappearance had compromised his mission. No doubt, somewhere his superior was highly annoyed with him and putting pressure on him to complete his assignment. That strain was the stress she saw in his eyes and felt emanating from him hot enough to burn—not desire for her, certainly not passion.

"I think...I need more time."

His eyes narrowed. "What are you saying?"

"I'm still just not sure. Marriage is such a big decision and I don't want to make a mistake."

"So, you are ending...us?" Anger, but not one hint of hurt suffused his tone. "This is goodbye?"

"No. No. No. I'm sorry." She raised her hands in the air and let them flutter helplessly to her lap, then warned herself not to overdo the theatrics. "I'm just so upset I'm not being clear."

"So you want to get married. That would be great. We can reschedule and—"

"No, Franklin. I'm saying I'm still not sure and want to give us more time."

His posture changed from stiff to stiffer. "How much more time?"

"As long as it takes?"

"I don't understand." He was probably attempting to sound confused but to her ears his tone came out strangled. "Are you having doubts about me? Or about yourself?"

"Both."

"What can I do to fix that?" His eyes projected kindness and a can-do attitude. Clearly, Franklin thrived on a challenge, and she couldn't help admiring his stick-to-it-ness that made it easier for her to continue as Web had suggested.

She figured she was doing okay. Holding up her end of the bargain with Web. She hadn't ended her relationship with Franklin and by the time he left, he'd agreed to "date" for a while until she could get a handle on her feelings. Step number one had been accomplished and she prayed the rest would go down just as easily.

"WE'VE GOT A PROBLEM," Web said after making sure the shades were down and greeting her with a kiss that told her though they'd only been separated for hours, it had seemed longer. And she was surprised at how much she'd missed him, wanting his arms around her and his kiss much more than his explanation.

Web kissed her thoroughly and pulled back reluctantly, admiration in his eyes. "You did great with Franklin. I was proud of you. If I hadn't known better, I would have thought you a professionally trained agent."

"Thanks." She hugged him, warmed by his praise, so happy to see him after the trying afternoon. Compared to Franklin, Web's honest praise was like taking a hot shower after coming in from the cold rain.

With a grin Web handed Kendall a bag of groceries, and she unpacked a flank steak, Idaho potatoes, salad greens, fresh asparagus and ice cream. Yet her thoughts weren't on food but on how much she'd missed seeing Web today. After Franklin had left, it had seemed to take forever until dark, until he could be certain no one was watching. As she waited impatiently for Web to arrive, she'd finished cleaning out her fridge and cleaning her home until it was spotless. She'd thrown an afghan over a lamp to soften the glow and drawn the shades. She fluffed the pillows on the couch, changed the sheets on the bed, regretting that she and Web couldn't make love because of microphones planted in her bedroom, so instead she dreamed of holding him, kissing him, talking to him.

And now that he was finally here, she couldn't take her gaze off his broad shoulders and massive chest. But best of all she could be herself once more. There was an ease between Web and her that had grown over the past few days. An ease that she appreciated all the more after the stiff conversation with Franklin.

After placing the ice cream in the fridge, she plucked a lighter from a drawer and tossed it to him. ''Grill's on the back porch.'' With her fenced backyard, they were safe from prying eyes and not even satellite surveillance of her home could penetrate the old wooden porch roof. ''What's the problem?''

Web headed out the back door and kept talking over his shoulder. ''After Franklin left, he went to the mall.''

Since the house was so small, she had no trouble hearing him as she rinsed and dried the vegetables, potatoes and makings of a salad. ''So?''

The gas grill huffed as he lit the burners. ''We think Franklin made a contact there.''

Kendall dried the potatoes with a paper towel, placed them on a plate and into the microwave but didn't turn it on. ''Web, I don't understand. Isn't that what we wanted? Isn't the plan to get Franklin to reveal his people?''

''Yeah, but we almost interrupted a legitimate operation. Franklin does lots of authentic work. So determining when he's on a real case for the FBI or on his own is going to be difficult.''

She took out a cutting board and began to chop celery and carrots. "We knew this going in, right?"

"Yeah."

"So, I'm confused."

"I should have said that Franklin has a problem." Web opened her fridge door and took out a bottle of barbecue sauce, then headed back with the steak in one hand, the sauce in the other. "With him involved in multi operations, he can't easily get out of town or take a vacation."

Placing butter in a frying pan, she added garlic salt and let the butter and spice simmer on low before adding the asparagus. "And?" she prodded.

"We have a lot of men tied up in this operation. The longer it goes on, the greater a chance of a leak."

"Are you worried about the expense?"

"No. If Franklin discovers we're watching him, he won't do anything at all and we won't catch him."

She tore apart leaves of lettuce and tossed them into a bowl. "How can I help?"

"We need to think of a way for him to get time off. Time to make a move."

"Can't his superior give him vacation time?"

"We don't know if his superior is in on his duplicity."

"Oh, I should have thought of that." She tossed the celery and carrots into the salad, added pine nuts, raisins and mandarin oranges from a can, and turned on the microwave. "Do you want me to suggest that we need to spend some private time together? I can't guarantee he'll agree. He's very picky about his work schedule. In fact it took him months to pick just the right date for our honeymoon.''

"I don't like the idea of you being alone with him. Of goading him into spending private time together,'' Web admitted.

"Why?''

"You know why.''

Web's tone was calm and firm. She had to remind herself that every word they spoke was being picked up by those microphones. She didn't have a stereo system, but her radio might mask their conversation. She turned it to a local country station, adjusted the volume higher than she would have normally, then joined him on the back porch. "If we whisper, can your friends hear us?''

He shook his head. "Not unless they turn over the tapes to an expert to clean out the background noise—which they won't do without a damn good reason.''

Reassured, she wrapped her arms around him and kept her voice low. "Did I tell you how much I missed you today?''

"Did you?''

She tilted back her head and locked gazes with him. "After Franklin left, I didn't feel clean. I let in fresh air and scrubbed the house and then took a shower, but until you arrived, I didn't feel like myself.''

"The thought of you with that bastard—''

"Don't.'' She placed a finger over Web's lips. "Don't do that to yourself. He didn't hug me or kiss me. Our only contact was when he touched my hand and I had to force myself not to jerk back.'' She shuddered and let Web see her distaste. "I'm not sure what I ever saw in him—except at the time he seemed safe.''

''For years he's fooled lots of people. Don't be hard on yourself.''

''It's not that.''

''Then what?''

''I want you to know that my feelings for you are nothing at all like—''

''Good.'' His mouth angled down over hers.

And the lights went out.

Chapter Twelve

"I've heard of powerful kisses, but not even yours should make the lights go out," Kendall teased.

"Very funny." Web took her hand. "From here I can't tell if the whole neighborhood is out or just your place."

"The rest of the meal is done, so whenever the steak is ready we can eat." She squeezed and released his hand. "I'll go find some candles."

Web surprised her by following her back inside. While she rummaged through the kitchen drawer, he peered at the neighbors who had also gone dark. His tone changed to serious. "With the electricity out, our monitoring equipment is dead."

"Are you implying the electricity outage is not an accident?"

"It's a possibility we have to consider." Web stepped to the back porch to check the steaks. "They're done."

She brought him a plate and he turned off the grill. "You think Franklin suspects that the Shey Group is watching me?"

"He may just be taking precautions. We'll still have warning if he decides to head out here. My cell phone is working.'' He surveyed the table set for two, picked up his plate, his glass and his silverware and placed them back in the cabinet, leaving the table set for one.

''Aren't you staying?''

''Yes. But do you mind sharing? I may have to disappear fast and don't want to leave any clues behind that you haven't spent the day alone.''

''You think Franklin's coming over here, don't you?''

''Yeah.''

Her appetite disappeared. ''You think he'll try to force me to leave?''

''It's too soon.'' Web must have heard the fear in her voice. Two steps within her small dining area and he had her back in his arms. She leaned into him, placed her cheek against his chest and just stayed there for a moment, feeling protected. Web's rock-solid presence steadied her. ''Franklin hasn't had time to make elaborate plans.''

''So what would be the point in showing up here unexpectedly?''

''He hasn't lasted as long as he has as an undercover agent without being careful. He may be coming over to test you, to try and trick you, to see how you'll respond to him when you aren't prepared.''

''Okay. I can deal with that.''

Web sat down and pulled her into his lap. ''Anytime you want out—''

''I don't.''

''You can still change your mind.''

''I'm not. I just didn't expect—''

''Franklin is cunning. He's going to try and surprise you. He's devious and underhanded—but never stupid.''

Kendall listened to Web, and although his words upset her, contradictorily, his presence soothed her. If she had to be bait, she'd rather play a more active role than sitting around and waiting for Franklin to make his move. But she supposed she didn't have much choice. As Web had already told her, waiting was the worst part of any operation and she totally agreed. Her mind had too much time to ponder every thing that could go wrong. She had to just go with the flow. Besides, if she suddenly became assertive, Franklin would question her motives more than he already did.

"I haven't changed my mind. I'm okay. Sorry I was so shaky for a minute there.''

"It's okay to be afraid,'' Web told her. "You'd have to be an idiot not to be. Every good soldier who goes into battle is afraid. Fear is nature's way of revving our biological engines, of keeping the senses sharp and the muscles ready for fight or flight.''

"You're scared?'' she asked, surprised that this bear of a man would admit such a thing.

"I'm terrified of losing you,'' he admitted. "But that's what's going to keep me sharp and on my toes.''

"Actually on your toes isn't exactly where I want you,'' she teased.

He chuckled, spanned her waist with his hands and gently set her back on her feet. "Don't tempt me, sweetheart. Now is not the time.''

She sighed. "Making love would be a great distraction.''

"Not if Franklin shows up," he reminded her.

"I'm not arguing—just protesting. I suppose I should feed you…"

"But you're not hungry?" he guessed.

"Nerves."

"Have a few bites and see if your stomach settles. You may find all that tension has left you starved but your body isn't reading the signals correctly."

She didn't believe him. When he sliced a piece of steak and fed her with his fork, she forced herself to chew and swallow. While he took the next bite himself, she sipped a cola. To her surprise her stomach was already demanding more.

"Another bite?" he offered.

"Are you always right?"

He placed another morsel between her lips. "I've had a lot of experience."

"So if you were Franklin, what would be your next move?" she asked as much to distract herself from the intimacy of the candlelit dinner as to prepare herself for what came next.

Web's eyes twinkled. "If I were Franklin, I'd definitely seduce you. But since he seems inclined to distance himself from his targets, I'd say he wants to see if you'll go off alone with him."

"And I'll protest a little and then agree, just like you instructed."

"Don't worry. Our guys are the best. Try and get him to say ahead of time where he intends to take you. It's better if we arrive before him and stake out the place instead of tailing him. But even if he won't commit to a destination, we'll be there for you. We have boats, an airplane and a helicopter standing by.

No matter how isolated you feel, you won't really
be alone.''

"Thank you."

"For what?"

"Reassuring me."

Web seemed to know exactly what to say to make
her feel better. And yet sometimes she wondered if
he, too, were playing her. Oh, she didn't doubt his
feelings for her. But as he said, he was experienced
at these spy games. And she had no doubt he could
be just as cunning and devious as Franklin.

Web's cell phone rang. "Yeah? Understood." He
flipped the phone shut. "He'll be here within five
minutes. Don't worry. While the electricity and
monitoring devices are out, I'll hide in the closet."

WEB SUSPECTED his close presence would help her
deal better with Franklin. Under the circumstances,
Kendall was doing remarkably well. She'd handled
Franklin just right the first go around. Still, she was
an amateur, and one mistake could put her life in
jeopardy.

Despite Web's proximity, Franklin could shoot
her before Web even had one whiff of suspicion she
was in danger. In fact, if Web hadn't believed that
Franklin needed Kendall alive and if the stakes
hadn't been enormous, he wouldn't have gone to
Kincaid with her suggestion. It was difficult enough
for experienced undercover agents who'd received
arduous training to pull off this kind of deception,
but for Kendall, who hadn't been taught how to deal
with the strain and tension, it was much harder.

Even if he hadn't fallen in love with her, her trust
in him and the Shey Group would have made him

both proud and determined to keep her safe. With his feelings so strong, he had to tamp down his emotions to do his job, but it wasn't easy. Before letting another woman grab his heart, he'd intended to discover beforehand if she was the kind of woman who could accept what he did for a living. But his feelings for Kendall had sneaked up on him. He had no idea what the future held for them, but no matter what happened between them, he meant to protect her with every fiber of his being.

As he climbed into the bedroom closet and left the door slightly cracked, he had a view of the living room and should be able to hear their conversation. He would have preferred to be closer, in the same room, but her living area had no hiding place. Settling against the back wall of the closet, he prepared to wait for as long as necessary. His position wasn't comfortable, but Web was accustomed to holding still for long periods of time if the job required it. And he could also extract himself soundlessly from the confines on the closet and close the distance to her within seconds.

However, it took less than a split second to throw a knife or pull a trigger. So although he made himself relax mentally, his muscles stayed tense, weapons ready if she needed him.

When Franklin knocked on the door, Kendall called out, "Who is it?" as if she had no idea who'd come calling. She really was good at undercover work, slipping into her role with the ease of a talented actress.

"It's me," Franklin answered in a voice Web would recognize anywhere. He had a way of pronouncing his words with extra clarity, no accent and a thread of hard undercurrents in his tone that made his diction unforgettable.

She unlocked the door, putting just the right amount of surprise in her tone. "Franklin?"

"I heard the electricity was out and came to check on you." Franklin entered the house, sniffing at the steak dinner and the candlelit table set for one.

"That was thoughtful of you."

"Steak and potatoes? Isn't that heavy food for your dinner?"

Web contained a groan, realizing that Kendall would have probably chosen pasta, fish or chicken for dinner. He also reminded himself that Franklin was a trained observer who depended on his instincts to survive. Luckily Kendall covered well.

"Mom loved steak and I thought I should use up what's in the freezer—especially with the electricity off for who knows how long."

"It should be back on soon," Franklin told her.

Did he come by that information from a phone call to the electric company or because he'd ordered the power turned back on? And if so, who had done his dirty work, and could the Shey Group connect him to the deed? On second thought, Web's people probably couldn't ask questions without revealing that they were watching the FBI agent.

"Well, I'm glad you came," Kendall told him as she scraped her plate and set the dishes in the sink. "Would you like some dinner? I could cook another steak on the grill."

"No, thanks. I ate right before the electricity went out." He shrugged. "Good timing, I guess."

Kendall filled the sink with soap and water. "I've

been thinking about us, about getting to know each other better.''

''And?'' Franklin came up behind her and spoke in her ear. Web didn't like the other man advancing so close to her. If anything bad went down, it lowered Web's chance of protecting her, but since he sensed no immediate danger, he just tensed, waited and listened.

At Franklin's sudden proximity, Kendall jumped a little but went on washing the dishes. ''I wish we could spend more time together. You work all the time.''

''I'm right in the middle of several important investigations for the IRS. We're trying to prove money laundering, racketeering and a Mexican connection that comes through Texas.''

Franklin had told Kendall he worked as an accountant for the FBI. And in truth this was his genuine cover that the Bureau had established for him. But Alabama wasn't exactly a hotbed of big-time crime, and Web figured Franklin had inveigled this assignment strictly for the purpose of meeting Christopher Davis's daughter—which seemed likely since Franklin had once been assigned to guard her father. The competent manner in which Franklin worked inside the FBI as a traitor infuriated Web, almost as much as the way he played fast and loose with Kendall.

''But if we'd gotten married,'' Kendall gently argued, ''we would have been on our honeymoon and you wouldn't have been working.''

Franklin's tone sharpened. ''We aren't on our honeymoon, are we?''

''My point was that since you'd planned to take

off this week before, why can't you do so now?''
Kendall finished washing and drying the dishes and
turned around, holding the dishcloth between her
and Franklin like a shield.

With her body language projecting exactly the opposite of her words, Web feared Franklin might
sense something was wrong. But as if realizing her
mistake, she tossed the dishrag aside, squared her
shoulders and tipped up her chin as if ready to do
battle.

Her tone was firm, insistent. "I want to spend
more time together. And I can't do that when you're
always working.''

"I'm here now. We could go for a drive,'' Franklin suggested, his voice once again silky smooth.

Web forced himself to breathe. He didn't want
them to leave. At least here in the house he could
monitor the conversation and stay close. Once they
went on the road and began to move, the operation
would turn dicey. As a trained agent, Franklin would
recognize any tail that came too close. They'd have
to switch off pursuit cars with a frequency that took
a lot of coordination and could allow for screwups,
especially on short notice.

"With the traffic lights down, I'd prefer to stay
here,'' Kendall told him.

Good girl. She'd come up with the perfect answer,
thinking fast on her feet and giving Franklin a reason
to remain here that was difficult to counter.

"Seriously, couldn't you arrange to take off a few
days?'' Kendall persisted.

"I already told you that my work is at a delicate
stage. Now is not a good time…''

She fisted her hands on her hips. "And when will be a good time?"

"I'm still saving my vacation for a wedding and honeymoon, but—"

"Oh, Franklin, you've just given me a terrific idea." Kendall's voice echoed with exuberance.

Uh-oh. Web had no idea what she was going to suggest. He had trouble getting past the wedding and honeymoon stuff with Franklin, but she hadn't mentioned any terrific plan to him. Whatever she was thinking, he wished she'd told him first. Clearly she was eager to force Franklin's hand. To get him to move on with his plan. Her idea of asking the man to spend more time with her might have accelerated the situation. But what was she up to? Web's gut clenched as he waited to hear what she would say next.

"What?" Franklin sounded curious.

"Why don't we skip the wedding and do our honeymoon?" Kendall said blithely, as if unaware that to Web her words would feel like a solid uppercut to the jaw.

What the hell was she thinking? Franklin and Kendall had been planning to honeymoon in Egypt.

Web had told her not to leave the house with Franklin and now she wanted to leave the country? Was she out of her mind? Leaving the United States would put her in enormous danger. Not to mention that she was implying she wanted to make love to Franklin!

Web's blood roared through his ears. He'd never expected her to do more than follow his directions, and he realized he'd lost control of the situation, something that seemed to happen all too often with

Kendall. Clenching and unclenching his fists, he fought for calm.

Franklin's tone turned bitter. "I canceled our hotel reservations."

Franklin must be feigning disappointment. Web understood he was simply pretending to object because Kendall had practically just delivered herself to him in handcuffs. But of course, if he seemed reluctant, Kendall might be all the more eager to go. She was too smart to fall for reverse psychology—though she would do so if it got her what she wanted.

"So, we'll make new reservations. Our plane tickets can be changed, and if there's a charge for altering the dates, I'll pay for that," Kendall offered. "Think, Franklin. This would be a chance to get away. To get to know each other much better." When she reached out and ran her finger up and down Franklin's chest in a sensual gesture, Web restrained a curse. He wanted to charge out of the closet and deck the other man.

Strict discipline kept him locked in place, barely breathing as he waited for Franklin's answer. The lights suddenly came back on, but Web felt as if darkness was choking him.

Head spinning with doubts, anger and worry over Kendall actually leaving the country, Web had difficulty steadying his thoughts. He forced air in through his nose and out through his mouth. Finally he reached a semblance of calm and concluded that once again he had let the green-eyed monster do a megatakeover inside his head.

Kendall hadn't so much as hugged Franklin. She hadn't kissed him. There was no sexuality between them at all. Web had better keep his head on straight and bury those jealous thoughts. Kendall simply wanted this mission to be over and done. She'd told him so. And now she'd forced the issue.

And in truth, besides putting herself in danger, her plan wasn't all that bad. By forcing Franklin to make a move, they would know what he was doing and when. They could check out the Egyptian hotel ahead of their arrival, plant a guide to take them to the sites, control the situation.

"Let me ask my boss for the time off and I'll see what I can do to parcel out my work."

"That would be great." Kendall ushered Franklin to the door and endured his peck on her cheek. "I can be ready to leave as soon as you give me the word."

As Web watched her smoothly get rid of the man, he buried his jealousy. She had enough to deal with without trying to reassure him. And deep in his heart he knew that she would never make love to Franklin. She simply wasn't that kind of woman. Open and honest, Kendall didn't play coy games.

Web trusted her to do what was right. And if things didn't work out between them, it wouldn't be because of Franklin. Her former fiancé had nothing to do with Web's feelings for Kendall, or hers for Web. If she and Web didn't stay together, it would be because Kendall didn't love Web. Nothing more. Nothing less.

As she locked the front door and Franklin's car pulled away, Web stepped out of the closet. She ran to him, flung herself into his arms. Icy cold and shaking, she held on to him with a death grip. And if he'd needed proof that she needed him, he had it. "It's going to be okay."

Chapter Thirteen

Kendall wished that Web could have spent the night, even if just so she could nestle against his warmth to sleep. But he had to return to the neighbor's house, clear her new plan with his boss and go over contingency options.

So he'd left her alone to toss and turn in her bed, unsure if she'd done the correct thing by suggesting to Franklin that they take their honeymoon. But the waiting for Franklin to do something had gotten to her. She'd wanted to act. She needed closure on the past in order to move on to the future.

She'd finally fallen asleep in the early hours of the morning to dream of Web. Web's arms holding her. His tone encouraging her. And she'd felt strong and powerful.

Then Franklin had invaded the dream. And she'd awakened with her heart pounding to the shrill sound of the telephone ringing. With a groan, she rolled over, reached for the phone and knocked it to the floor.

Damn. Damn. Damn. "I'm coming." She fumbled with the covers, her feet tangled in the spread. When she finally freed herself and answered, she was slightly out of breath. "Sorry, I dropped the phone."

Franklin sighed. "Can you be ready to leave by noon?"

"Noon?" She almost squeaked out the word. She'd told Franklin she could leave quickly, but she figured she'd have at least a day or two's notice. "Sure. Are we still flying through New York?"

"Yes. But you needn't worry about the details, all the reservations are taken care of."

"We are going to the same hotel?"

"It's a surprise."

Oh, no. Web wasn't going to like this at all. He'd wanted to make everything safe for her ahead of time, but if she didn't know where they were going, that wouldn't be possible.

"How long will we be gone?" she asked.

"Why?"

"I need to know how much underwear to pack."

"Plan on ten days. I couldn't get off for a full two weeks. This was the best I could do."

"I understand. And I appreciate what time you can give me." She winced as she said it, realizing how needy she sounded, but Franklin would expect her to be suitably grateful, so she was. "I'd better hang up and pack. See you soon."

In a flurry of activity, Kendall showered, brushed her teeth, then packed. Hoping Web would come over so she could talk to him one last time before she left, yet knowing he wouldn't risk it, in case Franklin had her home under surveillance, she tried to keep her mind on practicalities. Passport and visa, checkbook, sunscreen, reading material for their long airplane ride and lotion for her skin that always seemed dry at high altitudes. Kendall had never flown out of the country before. But she and her mom had once flown to Florida and gone to Disney World when she'd been eight. And she'd flown with her mom to see several specialists during the last year of her illness.

By noon, Kendall's stomach was clenched so tight, she feared eating anything. Aboard the plane, she tried and failed to read a magazine. Guarding herself constantly to prevent herself from craning her neck to search for Web, she nevertheless wondered if he was on her flight to New York. She didn't see him during a trip to the lavatory, but he could still be sitting up front in first class. Or he might have sent one of his cohorts. Or simply catch up with her in New York. Or Egypt.

"I didn't realize you were such a nervous flyer," Franklin commented, absently patting her hand.

"I'm not so much nervous about flying as excited about our trip. I've never been out of the country."

"Since you've never been anywhere," he sneered, "I hope you don't mind that I altered our plans."

"By changing the hotel?" She forced herself not to grip her seat's armrest too tightly. "No, I don't mind."

"We're not going to Egypt."

Her lower jaw dropped open. "We're not?"

"I thought your first trip should be European."

"But we don't have a visa."

"A visa isn't required in most European countries." Again he shot her one of his patronizing grins.

She tried not to think about Web, about how the

change in plans might throw off the Shey Group, who were expecting them to fly to Egypt and who might not realize until they failed to show up in Cairo that Franklin had changed their destination.

Making herself breathe, making herself ignore the nausea in her gut, she told herself the Shey Group had the wherewithal to track terrorists, and a simple change in flight plans wouldn't throw them off her trail. "So where are we going?"

Franklin opened his newspaper and smiled. "It's a surprise."

WEB RODE in a military aircraft that would arrive at a Washington, D.C., base and jet-helicopter him to Newark Airport, timing his arrival to land a full hour before Kendall and Franklin's plane. Through a headset, Web spoke to the Shey Group's premier computer specialist. Ryker Stevens's expertise was finding secrets through means legal and not so legal. Web wasn't concerned about Ryker's hacking through airline reservation systems to learn exactly where Franklin was taking Kendall.

"He's good," Ryker told Web with admiration. "He's used FBI resources to cover his bases. He has reservations into Stockholm, London, Barcelona, Cairo, Jerusalem, Rome and Munich. Since Stockholm and Munich would require a layover for the night, I'm ignoring them for now."

"What about hotel reservations in those cities?"

"He's probably made the reservation under an alias. Same with a car reservation."

Web heard typing as Ryker's fingers danced over a keyboard. "I'm checking FBI classified dossiers to find his aliases. Ah, yes. Franklin has duplicate passports in the last names of Henderson, Gere, Williams, Bonita and Tanner. He's requested an additional passport for his wife, Kelsey Tanner. Okay, we've got their names. He'll be making his reservations under the alias Richard and Kelsey Tanner.''

Web relaxed a little. "Good work."

"Standard operating procedure. I'll cross reference the names to every flight leaving Newark today in just a few minutes."

Web schooled himself to patience. No one was better at searching out information than Ryker Stevens. The man's computer genius was said to rival Logan Kincaid's—but the men specialized in different areas. Web had no doubt Ryker could discover their final destination, but time was of the essence. It was imperative to install their people before Franklin and Kendall arrived.

"Franklin's not planning on leaving out of Newark," Ryker informed Web, his tone certain. "He's booked a flight to London out of La Guardia. He has ten different connections from there." Ryker kept typing and talking at the same time. "Whoever's fronting him the money has plenty of it."

"Yeah. The stakes on this one could be billions." Web knew that Kendall was in the middle of a complicated international situation through no fault of her own, and he couldn't help admiring her for how she was handling herself. He just wished she hadn't had to put herself in danger to help her country. "The Middle-Eastern states don't like the idea of oil going down to ten cents a barrel, which could happen if Dr. Christopher Davis successfully completes his invention."

"Kincaid briefed me. He's sending in every man

he's got free to monitor, watch and assess. You're going to be fine.''

"Just tell me where he's taking her."

"I'm working the options." Constant clicking of the keyboard assured Web that Ryker was working at a furious pace. "Beside the flights out of Gatwick, he's rented a car, bought bus tickets for Glasgow and train tickets for Edinburgh."

Web shook his head. With the leaders of the U.S. and England so cozy, he doubted Franklin would feel comfortable promoting terrorism in a country so friendly with theirs. "My gut tells me he won't attempt to turn her over to terrorists in Britain."

"I agree."

"Beside all these travel arrangements, Franklin also made an interesting call to Greece. It was too short to trace to an exact location. He didn't bother to encrypt it, and what he said seemed innocuous, but we suspect it was a 'go' code."

Go meant the operation was starting. The best codes were the simple kind. Each contact would have a book of phrases. One person could say, "The weather is fine but it might rain tomorrow," and the listener could look up those words in their book and it might mean, "Meet me in Paris at the Louvre by noon." That kind of primitive code was virtually uncrackable without the accompanying cipher book.

Web had recently completed several missions overseas and was familiar with the political realities. "Greece is a hotbed of terrorist activity. Any chance that's his final destination?"

"Nope. I just got it. He's going to Barcelona."

"You know for certain?"

"For each leg of the journey, he used a different

name that matches his FBI passports. They are taking the train from London to Paris, flying to Madrid, then driving to Barcelona. And get this, his hotel reservation in Barcelona is for only one night.''

"You think the handoff will go down that quickly?'' Web asked.

"Yeah, but we'll be ready.''

Web hoped so, but in spite of the confidence he had in his fellow Shey Group team, he'd been in this business too long not to recognize how fast things could fall apart. And his worry over Kendall escalated.

AFTER THE LONG FLIGHT and then extensive traveling by assorted means of transportation, Kendall was exhausted. She'd never experienced Europe or jet lag before, and despite all the wonderfully intriguing sights out various windows, she could barely keep open her eyes. Unlike Franklin, who had slept most of the way over the Atlantic Ocean and seemed bright-eyed and alert, she wanted a shower, a bed and at least ten hours of sleep. Twelve would be better.

In an area on the outskirts of Madrid, Franklin stopped for gas and to buy her sunglasses and a hat. "I can't believe you forgot to pack them,'' he berated.

Too exhausted to argue or defend herself, when he returned with the items and plopped the straw hat and oversize glasses on her head, she didn't say a word. However, when he stopped at a crowed open-air market with interesting foods, leather goods and ceramics, she shook her head. "I'm too tired to shop.''

He turned off the motor, and heat invaded the vehicle. "We'll just get a bite to eat and be on the way."

"You go ahead."

"Come on." He walked her around the car and tugged her. The exotic spices, the vendors hawking their goods and the colorful cloths flapping in the breeze helped to awaken her. At any other time she would have paused to peruse the fine silver jewelry and leather goods, but she was practically in a walking stupor.

When Franklin passed one food stand after another, she planted her feet. Enough was enough. He'd dragged her across half of two continents and an entire ocean. She was tired and cranky and she wanted a shower.

Before she could say a word, a parade of dancers and musicians engulfed them on the street. One moment she was standing upright, the next, Franklin shoved her to the ground, knocked off her hat and snatched her sunglasses. Unaccustomed to the bright light, her eyes refused to focus. Then someone fell on top of her.

She shoved. "Get off me."

The man didn't budge. Short but muscular, with dark hair and brown eyes, the Spaniard blended right into the crowd. He pressed a gun into her side. "Do not speak, *señora*. Do not move or I shoot."

Fuzzy-headed, she didn't understand why the man wouldn't let her rise. Or why he had a gun pressed into her side. Were she and Franklin being mugged?

Craning her neck in a panic, she searched for Franklin. And the crowd parted. In that split second she saw him striding away with a woman dressed like Kendall. She wore a straw hat and the oversize sunglasses. Her hair color and style matched her own. If she hadn't known better, she would have assumed the woman was her.

Oh, God.

Franklin had just handed her over. As adrenaline surged with her fear, Kendall understood that Franklin had suspected all along that he was being watched. So he'd pulled off a switch right in front of whoever was watching. And even if she risked causing a fuss, if the gun hadn't deterred her, the music and singing would have. Even if she shouted, no one would hear. Real fear made her throat tight and her entire body tremble.

In all likelihood the Shey Group people tailing Franklin were no longer looking in her direction.

She was in a foreign country. In the hands of a terrorist.

With no one but herself to depend on.

Franklin had taken the bait, but she was the one who'd been caught. As the Spaniard jerked her to her feet, he wrapped an arm around her and jabbed the gun tightly into her side. Heart racing with fear, ribs flinching in pain, mind reeling from the sudden turn of events, she searched the street for a way to escape. For someone who might be sympathetic to her cause. But no one seemed to notice her plight.

She let her knees buckle, but the man carried her as if she weighed nothing. Within moments he shoved her into a van, climbed in after her and signaled the driver to go, talking in quick bursts of Spanish that she couldn't follow. However, she didn't need a translator to read the hostility toward her in her captor's eyes or his gleaming satisfaction at a job well done.

They had caught her. And she'd done nothing to stop them. Nothing.

In retrospect, she should have screamed. Should have taken her chances of being shot. Even now she should lunge for the steering wheel, yank the van from the road. But as much as she yearned to do something, anything, common sense prevailed.

She would pick her moment. Let them think she was cowed and too scared to fight. Let them laugh at their victory.

Web would be looking for her. He would figure out when Franklin had made the switch. He and his Shey Group would find her, wouldn't they?

And if they didn't?

She would find a way to help herself.

ALREADY INSTALLED in the room next to the one Franklin had reserved, Web frowned at Ryker Stevens. "They should have arrived by now."

Ryker opened one eye from the nap he'd been taking. "Traffic between Madrid and Barcelona is atrocious during rush hour." He checked his watch. "Wouldn't hurt to call our boys."

Web picked up the phone and lowered it slowly back into the cradle, the tiny hairs on his neck standing straight up. "No answer."

"When did you hear from them last?"

"An hour ago. Franklin and Kendall left an open-air market just outside Madrid and hit the highway— such as it is."

Web's cell phone, recalibrated for southern Europe, rang. "Yeah?"

Kincaid's voice was not the one he wanted to hear, and Web suppressed his disappointment that it wasn't Kendall on the line. "Spanish police just found both of Franklin's tails dead. We've lost Kendall."

Lost her?

Panic made his thoughts race. The police had made a mistake. Kendall would show up in the lobby any moment.

Stop it.

He didn't have time for denial.

Web relayed the information to the computer expert. "Ryker, see if you can pick up Franklin's location."

"He's gone to ground," Kincaid told Web. "One witness in the open-air market claims she saw a man force a blond woman into a white van."

"Did the witness get a license number?"

"The witness can't read. She's five years old. However, she insists that red balloons were painted on the side of the van."

"I'm on it." Ryker started typing. "But text searches are much faster than for logos. This isn't going to be quick."

"We'll find her," Kincaid said. "We're using all our resources. Interpol. CIA. With Franklin on the run, we can apply pressure."

And that pressure was considerable. "Thanks." Web ended the call and paced.

Franklin had planned this well. No doubt he had a nice, safe hidey-hole. And despite the combined resources of the free world, finding one man wasn't easy. Osama bin Laden and Saddam Hussein had both evaded searchers for long periods of time. Franklin was smart and could do the same.

Web calmed his rage by reminding himself that these terrorists needed Kendall alive. And they needed to trade her for Dr. Christopher Davis, her father. With that thought, he called Kincaid back.

"We may need Christopher Davis over here."

"Our government will not give him up to save his daughter."

"They can *pretend* the decision is up to Dr. Davis, can't they?"

"Letting him out of the country is out of the question."

"Damn it, Kincaid. Those terrorists have her. If they don't get what they want, they won't hesitate to kill her."

"Let me see what I can do."

Kincaid didn't lie to his men. He didn't soft-pedal bad news. But when he said he'd see what he could do, he'd move Congress, the Senate, the Cabinet and the joint chiefs of staff to do as he thought best. And it was rumored he nudged the president on occasion.

Ryker was typing furiously at work. Kincaid would pull every string in his command. Unfortunately, Web had nothing he could do—except wait.

But that wasn't good enough.

"If anyone needs me," he told Ryker, "I'm going to the open-air market in Madrid."

Chapter Fourteen

Lying down on the floor of the van with a terrorist pointing a gun at her shouldn't have been conducive to sleep. But from Kendall's position on the floor, she couldn't keep track of direction, couldn't watch the scenery, and after an hour of fighting to stay awake and alert, Kendall dozed, then fell into a deep sleep.

When she awakened to the rough nudge of the Spaniard's boot on her shoulder, she was still groggy. The van had stopped and the sun was setting. She estimated she'd slept for five or six hours. Not nearly enough.

In fact, after the man and driver escorted her into a dilapidated warehouse half-washed-away by what was probably the Mediterranean Sea, she wished she was still asleep. A quick glance around revealed her isolation. The exterior revealed nothing but overgrown weeds, a vehicle that appeared to have been junked in the middle of the last century and a half-submerged dock. Even if she could escape, she saw no place to run or hide. No nearby town. Nothing but a dirt road, miles of empty beach and the run-down warehouse.

That her captors didn't bother to tie her told her that they believed she couldn't escape, upping her anxiety a few more notches. In such a remote location, it was improbable that she would be spotted accidentally. Here there were no nosy neighbors. No curious dogs. No exploring children who might comment on strangers.

And no one could approach without being spotted from miles away. The land was flat, barren and, despite the setting sun, the temperature was quite warm. Sweat trickled between her breasts and under her arms.

Yet despite her perspiration, she shivered, knowing that this site could become her grave. The Shey Group couldn't know her location—not after Franklin's switcheroo in the open-air market. No group of commandos was going to land on this beach to save her. No SEAL team would miraculously swim out of the water. With no weapons except her brain, if she wanted to regain her freedom, she'd have to outwit her captors.

The Spaniard shoved her through an opening in the warehouse wall where a wide garage door might have once been. The odor of mildew and mold was almost overpowering, and she choked down her dismay. Sand had blown in through a multitude of holes that had once housed glass panes. The roof had fallen onto the metal rafters that were now inhabited by an assortment of critters. At their entrance, birds cawed angrily at being disturbed and flung themselves aloft before flying away.

Kendall didn't know if she preferred for the driver to stay or leave her alone with the Spaniard who had grabbed her from the open-air market. Two captors would be more difficult to evade than one. After the driver withdrew a bottle of tequila from his knapsack, twisted off the top and drank deeply before offering it to his cohort, she prayed they would get too drunk to take any personal interest in her.

Keeping her eyes downcast, she sat exactly where she was told to sit. She didn't move. She didn't speak, although her bladder desperately needed relief. Her plan was to blend into the rusting metal walls until the men forgot her presence.

To pass the time, she thought of Web. Knowing he was frantically searching for her with all the resources of the Shey Group made her feel less alone—connected, grounded. She wanted time to explore her feelings for Web, wanted time to see if what they had found was enough to build a lifetime together. Just because her father had abandoned his family and put his work first didn't mean that every man felt that way. She knew Web was different from her irresponsible father, and she was determined not to allow the emotional scars of her childhood stop her from finding happiness with a man.

As she sat in the damp sand, breathed the musty air, and as the men continued to drink, she searched her soul, wondering if one could ever separate the hurts of the past from the promise of the future. When she'd agreed to marry Franklin, there had been no emotional risk. Her heart hadn't been committed—so if he had left her—she would have been safe. But with Web her emotions were like a roller coaster. Up and down at a whirlwind pace. With Web there was emotional risk because she cared deeply about him. And she was afraid of the caring that made her so vulnerable.

As night fell, her captors polished off the bottle. They might not have been alert, but they weren't close to passing out drunk. When the driver headed to his car and returned with yet another bottle, a call of nature insisted that she could wait no longer.

Standing, she brushed off her hands and stood. "I must...use the lavatory." Of course there was no bathroom and the men seemed to find her words enormously amusing. They slapped their knees and laughed, paying her little attention as she slipped outside.

Quickly she took care of business. Was now the time to make her move?

If she ran, the men would come after her in the car. She wouldn't get far. She shook her head and went back inside, resumed her place by the wall. Better to wait for the right opportunity. She would only get one chance, and as she realized the men had drunk their way into the second bottle, she vowed patience.

Soon.

Soon she'd escape.

WEB HAD LITTLE TROUBLE tracking down the vehicle. The child witness's information proved accurate. After a visit to the local police station, he'd learned that a party van with balloons painted on the side had been stolen two days before. Another dead end. One of many.

Web returned to the open-air market. He had spoken to every vendor who hadn't yet packed up their goods for the day and gone home. No one had seen squat.

But someone was tailing Web. And that was the

best news yet. The fact someone was interested in him due to the questions he was asking suggested that person might know more than Web did. Or perhaps that person could lead him to someone who did. For two hours Web had let the man watch and follow him, waiting for an opportunity to turn the tables.

As Web played cat-and-mouse games with the stranger in the market, Ryker had kept in touch. So had Kincaid. Developments in the U.S. were interesting. Kincaid had not only managed to spirit Christopher Davis out of the top-secret government facility where he'd been hiding, the father Kendall had never met was now on a supersonic transport somewhere over the Atlantic Ocean.

Even more interesting, Franklin had contacted Dr. Davis on his cell phone and was demanding that the man turn himself over with his entire package of research or he'd kill Kendall. Franklin knew that the U.S. government didn't negotiate with terrorists, but had figured that Dr. Davis would be willing to pay to ransom his daughter.

Web suspected that if Christopher Davis was allowed to turn himself over to Franklin, the FBI agent would kill father and daughter, then resell the research material to the highest bidder. He steeled himself against how that eventuality would rip him apart. He loved Kendall. He wanted to spend the rest of his life with her.

Shoving aside the fear, downplaying the danger, Web concentrated on the problem of extricating Kendall from Franklin's grasp. Where had he stashed her?

If they'd caught a plane two hours ago, they could

be almost anywhere in Europe by now. Ryker needed to narrow down the search area. They needed a break.

Another hour later there was some good news. Ryker Stevens had broken Franklin's phone encryption, allowing the Shey Group to monitor his calls. The man was still in Spain. Even better, he'd phoned some very interesting cell phone numbers within the Saudi Arabian and Iranian governments—no doubt his contacts.

Kendall's plan to make Franklin reveal his network was actually coming to fruition. Web was proud of her and yet he was almost sick with the notion that Kendall was not going to survive. He'd let her down by failing to protect her. And now she was out there alone in a foreign land where she didn't speak the language, held captive by enemies who didn't treat their own women well, never mind strangers.

Web stepped into an alley and doubled back on the man tailing him. From the shadows of a recessed doorway, Web lunged out, slammed his follower into a wall. His surprised victim didn't struggle, but stared into Web's eyes as if assessing his character.

Holding one forearm against the man's throat, Web ordered, "Talk."

"I am Fernando Diaz, *señor. Policia.*"

"So?"

"So, I know something about the man who stole the van you were inquiring about earlier today."

Web didn't loosen his hold on the man's neck. "Why were you following me?"

"We needed to talk…in private. Not everyone in

our police department likes *Americanos, señor*. Your current president is not so very popular here.''

''And you like our president?''

''I approve of men of honor. Men like yourself. Men like your boss.''

Web raised his eyebrow, surprised Officer Diaz knew anything about the Shey Group or Logan Kincaid. ''My boss?''

''My father did a few favors for your countryman. Now I will help you and be well paid for my trouble. *¿Sí?*''

''What do you want?'' Web's suspicions escalated. He didn't like men who asked for bribes. That meant their loyalty went to the highest bidder and that they could not be trusted.

But Diaz surprised Web. ''I would like to be the Spanish contact for the Shey Group.''

Web thought over his reply. As eager as he was for information, he would not lie to this man. ''I cannot make any promises.''

Diaz's eyes searched his with calm as if he'd expected no more and no less. ''But you can see that I will be considered?''

''Yes. Now, what information do you have for me?''

''There have been a series of stolen vehicle thefts in Madrid. At first we thought the thieves cut up the cars, placed the parts in containers and then sold them overseas. But last week I heard about a driver taking the cars to a remote warehouse, loading the vehicles onto a tug, then transferring the vehicles to a ship at sea.''

''I am not interested in car theft.''

"Hear me out, *señor*. I believe one of the drivers is the man you are looking for."

"Why?"

"He has gambling debts and also a reputation for a willingness to do anything for fast cash. He is also missing from his usual bar stool. The man is very fond of drink."

"Back up a second. Why do you believe this man is the one I'm looking for?"

"The stolen van with the balloons was taken from his side of town, during the early-morning hours."

"That's not enough."

"The child's description fit him."

"The child's description could fit eighty percent of the men in Spain," Web argued. Although Diaz might be his best hope, he was not about to go running off in the wrong direction without more than this.

"I spoke to the child myself. He forget to mention in his first statement that the woman's abductor had an ugly ear."

"Cauliflower ear?" Boxers often had misshapen ear cartilage after taking too many punches. Web's hopes began to rise. "And this car thief has fighter's ears?"

"*Sí, señor.*"

"Do you know where he might have taken her?"

"Not for certain. But Samuel is not a complicated man. He comes from a small village on the coast. A village where locals keep their mouths shut about smuggling and are not friendly to city people or the *policia.*"

"You think he took her to the same place where he stashes the cars?"

''*Sí*, but this is what you call an educated guess. I am not sure.''

''Officer Diaz, would you be willing to accompany me on a search?''

''I would be honored.''

Web clicked open his cell phone and dialed. ''I need a chopper.''

KENDALL WAITED until her captors had almost finished the second bottle of liquor. One man was snoring and the other sat slumped, his eyes closed, the bottle loose in his hand. She had no doubt she could sneak away without them hearing her. But she wouldn't get far on foot.

She needed the car keys—car keys that must be in one of the driver's pockets. Her heart hammered up her throat as she shoved to her feet and fought to control her ragged breath. If the keys were in a back pocket where he was sitting, she didn't stand a chance.

Slowly, carefully, she edged closer to the driver. When he released a loud snore, she almost let out a yelp. There's no rush, she told herself.

You can do it.

All along she'd wondered if Franklin was working with others in the FBI. But if he'd had to resort to hiring undisciplined alcoholics to do his dirty work, he must be on his own. And she intended to use that to her advantage.

With two fingers she plucked back the snoring man's jacket pocket. But she found no keys in the right side. Nor the left side. Nor the front inside pocket.

Damn. They had to be in his slacks. Lucky for

her the pants were baggy. Before risking the maneuver of slipping her fingers into a pocket, she frisked him and found a hard lump, hopefully keys, in the right pocket. But although he was slumped, he was way too upright, the pocket's material kinked.

Risking everything, she placed one hand on his shoulder and shoved him over. He toppled gently, like a sleepy baby, but she held her breath, praying he wouldn't open his eyes. He didn't, but his lids fluttered.

She gave him a minute to go back into deep REM sleep. Then slowly she reached into his pocket and edged out the keys.

Adrenaline surged and every atom in her body goaded her to run. But instead, she made herself take the gun by his side before hurrying to the van, opening the door and slipping into the front seat. She didn't close the door for fear of making noise. Didn't turn on the lights in case the sudden brightness cast sleep disturbing shadows into the dilapidated interior. Kept the gun on the seat beside her.

The engine fired smoothly on the first try. She had a half tank of gas. Thank God, she knew how to drive with a clutch.

Shifting smoothly into first gear, she headed down the only road. She'd been sleeping on the way here. But with just one road, she felt confident she could get away and find a phone and help.

She had just reached to turn on her lights, when a motorcyclist roared out of the darkness. Her first thought was relief that Web had found her.

Then her van's lights flashed on the man's face.

God, no.

It wasn't Web but Franklin.

Chapter Fifteen

Franklin steered his motorcycle straight at her, as if playing a game of chicken. Blood blasting through her veins, mouth as dry as the sand her van skidded over, Kendall kept her foot on the gas pedal, both hands clenching the steering wheel.

The narrow dirt road had soft sand on the shoulders. If she turned aside, she might very well get stuck. Gritting her teeth, she held the center of the road.

She was in the bigger, heavier vehicle.

If they crashed head-on, she had the better chance of survival.

But sweat poured down her forehead into her eyes. Could she run over the man she'd once intended to marry?

Damn straight she could. Franklin had lied to her. Used her. Had her kidnapped and now the SOB was attempting to ruin her escape.

Don't turn the wheel.

Let him be the one to veer off the road.

When a helicopter's lights spotlighted her, she flinched. Was Franklin meeting her here to fly her to another location?

One problem at a time. Franklin aimed at her like a speeding bullet. In seconds they were going to collide head-on in screeching metal and vulnerable flesh. And in her rush to flee, she hadn't put on her seat belt.

Franklin was charging straight at her like an avenging demon escaped from hell. His bright headlight blinded her. The helicopter's spotlight shifted to the motorbike.

She would not break. Would not turn away.

Kendall closed her eyes. And prayed.

But the crash didn't occur. Opening her eyes, she stared at the empty road ahead, checked her rearview mirror. Franklin must have careened off the road at the last moment, circled around and was now giving chase.

She slammed her foot down on the accelerator, but she watched him gain steadily in her rearview mirror. In seconds he drew up alongside her. She yanked sideways on the wheel, attempting to run him off the road and the gun fell to the floorboards. Worse, her action only aided his effort to fling himself from the motorcycle to the van.

He'd dived through the window, and now his upper body rested on the seat, his legs dangling out.

"Stop the van," Franklin shouted at her.

She slammed her foot on the brake, then the gas, trying to dislodge him. But he had too much of his body inside the vehicle. However, the jarring motions prevented him from crawling farther inside, and he cursed her viciously as he clung to the seat.

The helicopter pinned her in its spotlight again, flying up her tail, hovering over the car, the blades creating a sandstorm, obliterating her view of the road. With Franklin inside the vehicle and the chopper overhead, her hopes of escape were dashed.

Still, she didn't give up, veering first right, then left until she feared she might flip over.

"JACK, CAN YOU SET the chopper down on the van's roof?" Web shouted, since he'd ditched his earphones and already had the helicopter's door open. Wind and sand shot through the chopper, making communication between the pilot and Web difficult.

"You'll have to jump," Jack shouted.

Web made a mental note to thank Jack's wife for sending him back into action so soon after their baby had been born. Jumping out of a chopper flying at an estimated fifty miles an hour onto the ground was risky, but trying to land on the roof of a moving van was one of the craziest stunts Web had ever attempted.

But Kendall was inside that van with a traitor.

Web stood on the skid, hung on to the landing gear. "Go right. More. Another two feet forward," Web directed, as Jack attempted to match speed and direction with the wildly veering van.

Web figured he could land on the roof, but whether he could cling to the surface after a jarring landing was doubtful. Still, he had to try. Help was on the way, more men, more vehicles and the local police, but Franklin was almost inside the van. Just his knees, calves and feet remained outside the window.

The van zigged right and the chopper zagged left. But just for an instant, Web was directly over the speeding van.

He jumped, took the impact on the balls of his

feet, then fell prone and spread-eagled, his wide-spread arms extending to the max, his fingers clutching to grab the roof rack, his weapon flying from the holster.

Got it.

He wrapped his fingers around tight. Just in time. She swerved and he almost pulled his arm out of the socket.

Ignoring the wrenching shoulder pain, Web slid over the roof and lunged into the van feet first. His limbs tangled with Franklin, and Web stomped down hard on the other man, hoping to nail him hard. Franklin shifted.

Kendall yelped in pain.

Franklin's twisting and turning to fight off Web must have hurt her.

Web's anger rose to a fever pitch. "Bastard. Try hitting a man for a change."

"Web?" Kendall's voice was filled with pain and surprise and fear.

Fury lent Web extra strength, but with no room to unfold his massive body in the tight space, he fought for leverage. Blows were of necessity short and tight. Wrapping one arm around Franklin's neck, Web tried to jam his fist into the other's chin. But his blow didn't land as he and Franklin slammed into the dash, the van crashing to a sudden halt in a ditch, tossing the men onto the sand.

Together the men tumbled, and Web's head ricocheted forward, then whipped back. He spit sand from his mouth, but although his shoulder hurt, he could clench and unclench his fingers and he never released his grip on Franklin's neck. Franklin might not have his musculature, but he was well trained and fighting for his life. He jammed his elbow into Web's ribs, tossed sand into his eyes.

The two men rolled in the sand, knees, elbows and fists landing blow after blow, but with neither man able to gain an advantage. During the struggle, Franklin broke Web's hold, then bent over his hand groping for his ankle. When he straightened into a crouch, he came up with a knife.

Web's foremost concern was Kendall. Had she been thrown from the van? Was she still inside it? Or was she somewhere on the sand where Franklin could reach her and use her as a hostage?

Training kept his attention focused on the weapon. Normally he'd block Franklin's knife hand, then grip and squeeze the wrist until his opponent was forced to drop the weapon. However, Franklin stayed out of reach, waiting for an opening to attack.

Web decided he'd have to use his feet.

"Web?" Kendall stumbled into view, the van's headlights revealing her dazed look and blood streaming down her forehead. She had a gun in her hand and was raising it to aim at Franklin.

"Stay back," Web ordered her.

Franklin edged toward Kendall. Web lunged with a roundhouse kick, his foot arcing, then coming down on Franklin's wrist. At the same moment, Kendall fired the gun. Franklin's knife went flying, but he spun and thrust himself at Kendall, knocking her backward, and her second shot went wild.

But anticipating his opponent's move, Web kicked out again, catching Franklin on his temple. He let out a woof of air and collapsed. Out cold.

Then Kendall was bending over Franklin. At first Web thought she was concerned, but then he glimpsed the gun she held on him, her eyes fierce. "My first shot only got him in the shoulder. I ought to kill him."

"Don't." Web took the gun from her hand, flicked on the safety, then tucked it into his jacket. "We need the intel our boys will sweat out of him."

With the helicopter landing, Web placed his arm over Kendall's shoulder and drew her close. "You okay?"

"Yeah."

"They didn't hurt you?"

She turned into his chest and snuggled. "I knew you would come get me."

"It's my job."

"I'm glad." Her eyes glimmered with tears of relief and happiness.

"You don't mind what I do for a living?"

"Mind? You just saved my life. Why would I mind?"

"But how will you feel when I have to leave you behind to help someone else?"

"I'll be glad that you have a good team behind you. I'll be glad that you're so strong."

That she could accept him so completely caused his heart to swell with love. She might not know it yet, but she was going to be his. He vowed to be patient, to give her time to understand that he might leave her, but unlike her father, Web would always come back to her. As much as he wanted to keep her all too himself, he couldn't do that, not with someone else waiting for an introduction.

"I have a surprise for you," Web told her. "There's a man in the chopper I want you to meet."

"He can wait," she muttered, tipping up her

mouth for a kiss. She tasted so good he never wanted
to let her go. But finally he made himself pull back.
"He's waited long enough. It's your father."

"MY FATHER?" Shock and excitement made thinking difficult. When Franklin had slid through the
truck's window, she'd been sure she was about to
die. Then Web had swooped down like some avenging hero to save her, and before she could quite comprehend that she was safe, the moment she'd anticipated for her entire life was upon her.

She was going to meet her father.

Christopher Davis jumped out of the helicopter,
rushed to her, then halted in the sand three feet
away, seemingly unable to close those last steps. Unsure of his welcome. Her father had aged well, looking much like the picture Web had shown her of him
in his laboratory. He had her eyes and mouth, a nose
totally long and straight that shared no resemblance
to her own. But what caught at her heart were the
tears streaming down his face.

His voice was choked up and husky. "Thank God,
you are safe."

"Thank Web," she replied flippantly, her sarcasm
and defenses going up. "Why are you here?"

"To offer myself in your place with the terrorists."

She didn't understand. This was the father who
had never sent a birthday card. Never once phoned
to speak to her. And suddenly he was willing to give
his life for her?

He must have read the confusion in her eyes. "I
haven't been a very good father."

"You haven't been a father at all." Years of hurt

at being ignored hardened her to him. He'd always put his work before his family, so she couldn't quite believe he'd been willing to risk his neck to save hers.

Web squeezed her hand. "He has every intention of making up for that lack."

"I'm not good with people." Christopher spoke sadly. "I thought Franklin was my friend. When I told him about you, I didn't realize I was putting you in danger. I get so caught up in my work that I forget security. I even forget everyday matters like, like—"

"Having a wife and child?" she muttered.

Web gestured for Jack Donovan to place Franklin in handcuffs before carrying the injured traitor to the chopper. "Kincaid had to pull strings to get Dr. Davis over here."

"Call me Chris."

"However, after your father heard about the danger you were in," Web continued, "he slipped past his handlers and offered himself to save you."

"Why?" Her throat choked on the word. She'd always imagined that her brilliant father considered her no more than his sperm gone awry. And she'd imagined all kinds of ways of meeting him, from his showing up at her high school graduation as a surprise guest to even his begging her forgiveness at her mother's funeral. But never would she have imagined circumstances this bizarre.

"My invention is complete. We still have to modify the design for ships, airplanes, trains, submarines and…but…other men can do that. I was the one who could save you—so I came."

Simple words. Astonishment, confusion and shock

swirled into a tempest of emotions that blasted her into stillness. In his own way Christopher Davis loved her. The father who had totally ignored her his entire life loved her. She heard it in his somber voice, saw it in the uncertain way his eyes kept reaching out to hers, then glancing away in misery. But most of all she felt it in her gut. And Web had taught her to trust that gut instinct. Her father had crossed the Atlantic to give his life for hers if necessary. The least she could do was take the last three steps to him.

Seemingly of their own volition, her feet brought her to him. And then she was hugging him. "Thank you for coming here."

"I want you to understand that I put the priority of my country first. Most people consider that wrong. But that is why I never…"

"Mom told me." And Kendall hadn't believed her, hadn't wanted to believe that his work was more important to him than his daughter. She didn't know if he intended to disappear back into his laboratory and never come out again. While she would like to get to know her father, her self-confidence and self-worth no longer depended on his decision.

Over her father's shoulder she shot Web a smile. The danger was finally over. They'd made it through safely, and Franklin was in custody. The Shey Group would round up his cohorts in other countries. Most important, they could all go back to their normal lives. And hers would include Web.

Epilogue

One Year Later

Kendall smoothed the bodice of her wedding dress before her mirror. Who would have thought that Dr. Christopher Davis would be taking time out of his busy schedule to walk his daughter down the aisle? Certainly not her. But in the year since they'd met, a bond had formed. Her father might let weeks go by between phone calls, he might have only flown to Alabama once; but she'd gone to visit him at his laboratory. He was now part of her life and she part of his.

However, her father was not the most important man in her life. Web Garfield held that spot of honor. Though she'd been slow to commit to love and marriage, Web's steadfast belief in her, his willingness to back up her plans to finish school had won her over. Looking back on the past year, she realized that Web and she were meant for one another.

Web was the right man. Yesterday. Today. And tomorrow.

With a smile of happiness, Kendall walked down

the aisle beside her father. Up ahead Beth waited, her eyes approving. That her best friend liked Web made Kendall feel doubly certain that agreeing to marry him was the best of decisions.

Warm and tender, Web's eyes never left hers, sending a special shimmy straight through her. She didn't know how she'd gotten so lucky to have this man's love, but she intended to cherish him always. She might have been slow to come around to admitting to herself that she loved him, but she couldn't have been more certain of her feelings. She loved Web with all her being and couldn't imagine life without him.

"You look good enough to eat," Web whispered as he took her arm.

"Web!"

As she blushed, eager for their wedding night, he chuckled knowingly. "It's okay to want me, sweetheart. I love you."

She would never tire of hearing those words. And now she could say them to him freely, without reservations, her heart happy and full.

"I love you, too. Now shut up and marry me, darling."

For a sneak preview of at the next book in Susan Kearney's HEROES INC. *series,* Protector S.O.S, *to be published in October 2005, please turn the page.*

Protector S.O.S
by
Susan Kearney

"You're late," Sandy Vale's eccentric millionaire client complained, his tone filled with annoyance, his wrinkled jowls sagging at his throat.

When Sandy and her first mate, Ellie, delivered new sailboats to their buyers, most of them beamed from ear to ear. But not Martin Vanderpelt. He frowned, his lips pressed firmly together, as if he already knew that he would find something to complain about.

Sure that the cabin was shipshape, Sandy hopped off the deck, tied the bow line around the cleat on the dock, then straightened and tried to ignore Martin Vanderpelt's scowl. "We ran into a little rough weather, sir. Nothing your boat couldn't handle."

Ellie positioned bumpers between the boat and the dock to protect the hull from scrapes, and Vanderpelt's glance lingered over Ellie's tanned legs. "For the money I paid, I expected your delivery to be on time."

"Sorry you had to wait, but I think you'll be pleased. She's a beauty, Mr. Vanderpelt." Sandy held out her hand in a friendly manner, pretending she didn't notice the coldness in Vanderpelt's expression. After several weeks at sea, she normally enjoyed landfall, but as clouds scudded over the sun and the air temperature dropped ten degrees, Vanderpelt ignored her handshake and climbed aboard the thirty-six-foot vessel, and Sandy wished she was back at sea.

She didn't like the way Vanderpelt had looked at Ellie. Not that lots of men didn't look at her friend, but there was something cold in his eyes that warned her he hadn't made all his millions by being a nice guy.

Reminding herself that Vanderpelt wasn't just any client and that she needed his goodwill, after he refused her handshake, she bit back her sarcastic, "So pleased to meet you, too." She couldn't afford to mouth off—not when Vanderpelt had bought a half-dozen sailboats for his wealthy guests to race around the island. Despite the rumors about Vanderpelt's rude manners, Sandy and Ellie hoped for repeat business. However, while they might not be chosen to deliver Vanderpelt's next boats, it would be worse if he complained about their service to the boat manufacturer who'd hired them.

Ellie and Sandy needed the extra money they earned delivering boats to their new owners to help support their fledgling marina. Okay, maybe not so fledgling. They'd expanded over the past two years, adding a lucrative retail supply business to their main operation of leasing slips and selling fuel. They no longer worried over paying their bills, but they had more plans for another expansion in the works.

Vanderpelt headed down below, and Ellie rolled her eyes at the sky, signaling what she thought of the high-and-mighty Vanderpelt. Sandy shrugged.

During the past year they'd had other unusual clients. A buyer in Florida had met them on his dock in his pajamas, a glass of champagne in his hand and a buxom blonde under each arm. A movie star in L.A. had burst into tears at the sight of his boat, totally overcome at finally being able to afford the yacht he'd always dreamed of. Sometimes Sandy felt like Santa Claus—but not today.

She distracted herself from Vanderpelt's displeasure by perusing his private island. Located about a hundred miles due east of Nova Scotia and part of Canada, the forbidding rocky shoreline and chain-link fence around the perimeter with No Trespassing signs posted every ten feet looked more like a military compound than the luxurious home of an eccentric millionaire.

A stately two-story house with a steeply pitched roof perched on tall pilings next to a clearing that looked like a helicopter pad. Vanderpelt's pilot was supposed to fly them back to Bar Harbor, Maine, where they could rent a car, head home and regroup before heading out to sea again.

Vanderpelt's thinning blond head poked out of the cabin followed by the rest of him. Sandy hoped his expression would have lightened to pleasure after seeing the rich mahogany cabinetry, the immaculate galley and the well-appointed cabin, decorated by a top Toronto designer.

But his blue eyes had narrowed, and the furrow between his brows had deepened to a fierce glower. "This is not my boat."

Sandy and Ellie exchanged uh-oh glances. Although Sandy's concern was intensifying with the storm blowing in, she kept her voice pleasant. "Mr.

Vanderpelt. Lightning struck the mast of your boat and melted part of the hull. The manufacturer wanted you to have a brand-new, undamaged boat. You're lucky they had a replacement.''

"You brought me a substitute? That's not good enough. It's unacceptable," he sputtered.

Sandy kept her tone businesslike to cover her annoyance. The customer wasn't supposed to know that his original boat had been damaged, but obviously someone had screwed up either the design or the decor, cluing him in to the switch. "Sir, if you have a beef with the manufacturer, I suggest you call them. I'm a subcontractor. I was paid to deliver this boat to you. If the boat's unsatisfactory, you need to take that up with Danzler Marine. Not me.''

"Damn right. You wait right here.'' Vanderpelt stalked off, his cheeks and jaw flushed with rage.

"Like we're going anywhere," Ellie muttered. "There's not another piece of land within a day's sail.'' She glanced at the dark cumulus clouds rolling in. "I think I'd prefer facing the storm and the sea to his mood.''

"Hang on. We'll be out of here soon enough.''

"I've got a bad feeling about him.'' Ellie shivered and glanced over her shoulder at Sandy, her usual dancing green eyes dimmed.

Sandy sighed. "I never understood why Danzler Marine didn't tell Vanderpelt up front about the lightning, but now I know. They didn't want to deal with his temper.'' Sandy straightened her spine. "Keep in mind that he's so rich, he's probably accustomed to his every whim being catered to. When something goes wrong, he has all the self-restraint of a two-year-old.''

Vanderpelt returned shortly with another man at his side. His cohort was about five foot ten, with dark, thinning hair, heavy-lidded eyes and tan skin that suggested he spent a lot of time outdoors. His obsequious manner suggested he was an employee rather than a guest. One look at his stoic face suggested to Sandy that the man was all business and accustomed to Vanderpelt's rages, but what bothered her most was the bulk under his jacket.

"What's up?" Sandy asked, a lump of fear lodging in her gut. Ellie's brother Travis had worn jackets that bulged under the arm. Like Travis, this man was carrying a weapon. Unlike Travis, he had a shifty look to him. And the fact that Vanderpelt had brought muscle didn't bode well for Sandy and Ellie.

Vanderpelt raised his voice to be heard over the rising wind, the clanging halyards and the waves lashing the dock. "There's been a change of plans. You and Alan will return this boat and sail back in the one I ordered."

"Sorry, we don't take passengers." Sandy tried to politely refuse to take Alan.

Vanderpelt shook his head. "He won't be a passenger, he'll be crew."

"Ellie and I can handle the boat by ourselves. We sailed her here, we'll sail her back, together." And that couldn't be soon enough. Sandy untied the front cleat. As if reading her mind, Ellie started the engine.

That's when Alan drew his gun. He spoke with no inflection and a British accent. "Ellie is staying with Mr. Vanderpelt as his guest. So you'll be needing me for crew, after all."

He stepped aboard and motioned with his gun for

Ellie to debark. Eyes wide with fear, Ellie stared at Sandy, silently begging her to help her.

Oh…my…God. Vanderpelt was keeping Ellie as a hostage. And with the weapon trained on her friend, there was not a damn thing Sandy could do to help her.

researching the cure

The facts you need to know:

- **One woman in nine** in the United Kingdom will develop breast cancer during her lifetime.

- Each year **40,700** women are newly diagnosed with breast cancer and around **12,800** women will die from the disease. However, survival rates are improving, with on average 77 per cent of women still alive five years later.

- **Men can also suffer from breast cancer**, although currently they make up less than one per cent of all new cases of the disease.

Britain has one of the highest breast cancer death rates in the world. Breast Cancer Campaign wants to understand why and do something about it. Statistics cannot begin to describe the impact that breast cancer has on the lives of those women who are affected by it and on their families and friends.

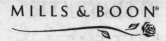

MILLS & BOON®

**During the month of October
Harlequin Mills & Boon will donate
10p from the sale of every
Modern Romance™ series book to
help Breast Cancer Campaign
in *researching the cure.***

Breast Cancer Campaign's scientific projects
look at improving diagnosis and treatment
of breast cancer, better understanding how
it develops and ultimately either curing the
disease or preventing it.

Do your part to help

Visit <u>www.breastcancercampaign.org</u>

And make a donation today.

researching the cure

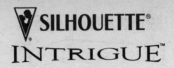

SILHOUETTE®
INTRIGUE™

THE COWGIRL IN QUESTION by BJ Daniels

McCalls' Montana

Despite Cassidy Miller's pleas of innocence, Rourke McCall still held his old flame accountable for murder. But as their feelings for each other rekindled, he suspected their relationship had made her the murderer's next target.

NOT-SO-SECRET BABY by Jo Leigh

Top Secret Babies

Jenny Granger had escaped a psychopath, but now he'd kidnapped her son and bribed her back into his clutches. Nick Mason had helped Jenny before, and was determined to save her again.

PROTECTOR S.O.S by Susan Kearney

Heroes, Inc.

Travis Cantrell had two things on his mind: rescuing his sister from a madman, and dealing with the overwhelming desire he had for her best friend, Sandy Vale. Would Travis and Sandy succumb to the ultimate temptation?

THE MAN FROM FALCON RIDGE
Rita Herron

Eclipse

To escape her past, Hailey Hitchcock had fled into the arms of sexy stranger Rex Falcon. Hailey's recollections of a murder send chills down his spine. And as threats aroused their forbidden desires, would the killer bury the truth?

Don't miss out!

All these thrilling books are on sale from 16th September 2005

Available at most branches of WHSmith, Tesco, ASDA, Borders, Eason, Sainsbury's and most bookshops

Visit our website at www.silhouette.co.uk

FREE! 2 Books and a surprise gift!

We would like to take this opportunity to thank you for reading this Silhouette® book by offering you the chance to take TWO more specially selected titles from the Intrigue™ series absolutely FREE! We're also making this offer to introduce you to the benefits of the Reader Service™—

★ FREE home delivery
★ FREE gifts and competitions
★ FREE monthly Newsletter
★ Exclusive Reader Service offers
★ Books available before they're in the shops

Accepting these FREE books and gift places you under no obligation to buy, you may cancel at any time, even after receiving your free shipment. Simply complete your details below and return the entire page to the address below. You don't even need a stamp!

YES! Please send me 2 free Intrigue books and a surprise gift. I understand that unless you hear from me, I will receive 4 superb new titles every month for just £3.05 each, postage and packing free. I am under no obligation to purchase any books and may cancel my subscription at any time. The free books and gift will be mine to keep in any case.

I5ZEF

Ms/Mrs/Miss/Mr ....Initials ....
BLOCK CAPITALS PLEASE
Surname ....
Address ....

....

....Postcode ....

Send this whole page to:
UK: FREEPOST CN8I, Croydon, CR9 3WZ